ELEKTRA

A NOVEL BY YVONNE NAVARRO
BASED ON A MOTION PICTURE SCREENPLAY
STORY BY ZAK PENN AND STU ZICHERMAN
& RAVEN METZNER
SCREENPLAY BY ZAK PENN

POCKET STAR BOOKS
New York   London   Toronto   Sydney

The sale of this book without its cover is unauthorized. If you purchased this book without a cover, you should be aware that it was reported to the publisher as "unsold and destroyed." Neither the author nor the publisher has received payment for the sale of this "stripped book."

This book is a work of fiction. Names, characters, places and incidents are products of the author's imagination or are used fictitiously. Any resemblance to actual events or locales or persons living or dead is entirely coincidental.

An *Original* Publication of POCKET BOOKS

A Pocket Star Book published by
POCKET BOOKS, a division of Simon & Schuster, Inc.
1230 Avenue of the Americas, New York, NY 10020

™ and © 2005 by Twentieth Century Fox Film Corporation and Regency Entertainment (USA), Inc. (In the U.S. only)

™ and © 2005 by Twentieth Century Fox Film Corporation and Monarchy Enterprises S.a.r.l. (In all other territories)

ELEKTRA character likenesses ™ and © 2005 Marvel Characters, Inc. All rights reserved.

All rights reserved, including the right to reproduce this book or portions thereof in any form whatsoever. For information address Pocket Books, 1230 Avenue of the Americas, New York, NY 10020

ISBN: 1-4165-0505-9

First Pocket Books printing January 2005

10 9 8 7 6 5 4 3 2 1

POCKET STAR BOOKS and colophon are registered trademarks of Simon & Schuster, Inc.

Manufactured in the United States of America

For information regarding special discounts for bulk purchases, please contact Simon & Schuster Special Sales at 1-800-456-6798 or business@simonandschuster.com.

For
Nora

Thank you to:

Christopher Golden (again)

Jennifer Heddle

Weston Ochse

Martin Cochran

Hitomi Withers, for help
with Japanese translation

Jason ErskinE

Kuljit Mithra of
www.manwithoutfear.com

and

Glen of the Technology Nook in
Sierra Vista, Arizona,
who kept me going with borrowed parts when
my computer blew up.

Prologue

HELL'S KITCHEN, NEW YORK

EVEN IN NEW YORK, THERE ARE MOMENTS AND places of silence, not minutes but slivers of time where nothing—man, animal, rodent, or machine—moves, where even the wind seems to hold its breath.

Of course, these moments seldom last very long. After all, this *is* New York.

Somewhere in the city—in *most* of the city—neon and fluorescent lights flickered and buzzed, bathing the streets, buildings, and a hundred thousand late night partygoers in false, multicolored daylight. Music spilled from the doorways of clubs and shops in never-ending waves of sound, booming, whining, sometimes floating along the layers of cigarette smoke and pollution like something that might have been beautiful had it not been overwhelmed by its surroundings, swallowed up in the raw power of New York City's nightlife. In this ocean of light and sound and movement, the lives of people small and great were lived, their deaths were planned and experienced and sometimes even avoided, and all the while the common people remained utterly ignorant that only a few streets over, entire destinies were being changed.

An ambulance, large, boxy, and top-heavy, careened around the corner onto a nameless residential street where the incessant glare of neon had been replaced by lights spaced too far above to be of any use. Its bright headlights cut across the darkness, painting a solid stream of brightness where the red and white revolving bubbles across the top of its cab blinked and disappeared, blinked and disappeared. The only thing that moved in its path was a crumpled piece of newspaper sucked across the road just ahead of its bumper. Puddles of oily water fountained from beneath the vehicle's tires, but there was no one around to splash. Dim lights burned here and there in the windows of the apartments overlooking the street, but the people inside, secure in the dubious safety of their homes, had long ago grown accustomed to the sudden shrieking of ambulance sirens; they paid little attention as the driver of this one leaned forward and flicked the switch back and forth.

Supplies rattled wildly in the side racks as the ambulance hit a pothole and bounced. The two paramedics in the back noticed only enough to grab at the IV hooked on one inside wall and keep it from jouncing off the wall hook. A heart monitor bleeped erratically, then went into alarm mode—

beeeeeeeeeeeeeepppppp!

"She's crashing!" Ray, the younger of the two, bent over the lovely young woman on the cart and yanked up first her left eyelid, then the right. There was a wide, shallow cut high on the left side of her neck that looked like someone had tried for her carotid artery, but this bothered him not at all. But her stomach was something else, and crimson blood oozed from beneath her back despite the heavy pack of bandages they'd put under her to try to slow the bleeding. The bandages were pressed tightly against a puncture wound made by some kind of wide and vicious blade that had gone all the way through her body. Even so, there was no time to be gentle. He'd gotten a little bit of response from his earlier check of her vitals, but now her pupils were fixed, dilated wide, and dark. There wasn't much time.

Bob had twenty years of experience at this job, so he didn't need to be told what to do. He reached over the woman's body and snatched a portable defibrillator off the wall at the same time Ray yanked the sides of the top of their patient's costume open as far as he could. Her black top was some sort of shiny leather halter thing that looked like it would be more at home at a Halloween party, or maybe one of those fetish raves, and it made the two electrodes he'd stuck onto the skin of her upper chest look stark and out of place. There was more leather—full-length gloves and a strap, cut through and dangling from around her neck. Finding a pulse had been difficult; they'd done it, but now that fleeting indicator of life was gone. Under any other circumstances, the two medics would have fully appreciated the woman's lovely face and gorgeous body, but the blood soaking her midsection blew away any such thoughts.

There was a barely discernible background whine that the practiced ears of both men recognized, and within seconds of turning it on, Ray yanked his hands away. As he pressed the paddles against her bared skin, Bob yelled *"Clear!"* anyway, following his ingrained training protocol. He pressed the buttons on his two paddles simultaneously, and the machine made an oddly low-key *whumping* noise at the same instant the young woman's body arched and rose a good six inches off the sheet.

Nothing.

"Again!" yelled Ray. He snatched the paddles from Bob and waved them in the air. "Come *on*, lady!" Bob jabbed a stiff finger at the *Charge* button on the side of the defibrillator; he had to aim at it twice because of the swaying of the ambulance. Another high-pitched whine as the machine again built power, and the instant the ready light came on, Ray again jammed the paddles against the bared skin of her chest. *"Clear!"* the

4

medic shouted, but once more his partner had already raised his hands.

The jolt made their patient's body arch again, but the movement went almost unnoticed in the bouncing of the ambulance. She fell back onto the blood-soaked sheet of the cart, and both of them bent over her, searching for a pulse, a tick of her eyelid, *anything*. As Bob pressed his stethoscope against her breast, one slender and strangely calloused hand slid over the side and banged lifelessly against the rubber-coated floor.

The older paramedic sat back. "She's gone," he said. His shoulders slumped in defeat and he swiped at his damp forehead with the back of his forearm. Ray scowled and looked like he wanted to try again, then the paddles he was still gripping slowly lowered. After a moment, he exhaled and nodded, finally slipping the paddles back onto their hooks. Now that the frantic moments were past, he could see that the woman's sightless eyes were open about a quarter of an inch; they were sort of a swamp brown color with highlights of green, and still bright enough to look alive—God, but she had been beautiful. He let a few more moments pass, then he reached out and gently pressed down on her eyelids to close them for the last time.

1

JAPAN

THERE ARE SOME WHO SAY THAT THE DESTINY OF each and every person is preordained, that there is lit-tle—or nothing at all—that the average person can do to change his or her fate. Save a man from stepping in front of the bus that was meant to end his life, and that same man will slip in the bathtub the next morning and split his skull. Philosophers throughout the cen-turies have likened it to the grand old game of chess, where each move is planned far in advance based on the possibilities at hand. A poor comparison, because it is one which makes the assumption that the focus of the challenge, the players, actually *know* which paths are available and what might happen when each road is chosen. But life, it seems, is much more like the an-cient Japanese game of Go, where even the best of players can sometimes find themselves seriously trapped and unable to break free, even beyond the death of a playing piece. Go, unlike life, assumes two sides with equally matched opponents. Some might say it's good against evil, but it's never truly that simple. Life is that game of Go, always going on around us, everywhere we turn or think to turn, in every choice we make, every step we take.

The ancients whisper to one another that secret portions of the game are real, that somewhere there are actual competitors, and that everything in the lives of the players in this mystical game continues from a challenge match of Go started five hundred years ago in Japan. They talk in hushed tones about how it began in a medieval Japanese village where the clan wars had finally ended and an entire generation of samurai suddenly found themselves with little or no livelihood, no way to feed and support families and wives, no means to provide dowries for daughters waiting to be wed. Life for them became an existence of anger and boredom.

As is often the case—or again, so they say—idle hands are the playground of the devil, and so they turned to the villagers for entertainment and sustenance. The languishing *ronin* robbed and pillaged and committed other acts considered unspeakable, and soon the powerless villagers searched for other methods with which to defend themselves. They turned to stealth and secrecy, and ultimately found their salvation in mastery of the mystical arts. Surprisingly, it wasn't that long before the last of the masterless samurai were defeated.

Knowledge, however, had taken a firm hold, and

over the years these humble villagers grew into a large and powerful organization. What had started out of necessity as a militia to protect the people turned into a dark and criminal enterprise, a *yakuza* powered by forces the average man would never understand. They called it *the Hand*. Its practitioners hid their faces behind the black costumes of ninjas, and the rare witness to a Hand member's death whispered of the acrid green smoke that wafted from the body when its spirit went on to its reward . . . or punishment.

The Hand grew strong, *too* strong. Ruthless, cruel, *barbaric*—they evolved into exactly what they had been created to defeat. Their darkness blossomed like kudzu and took over large parts of the underworld until even the hushed mention of their name brought shudders of dread.

But things have a way of balancing out.

For every black deed, there is a white one, for every evil created, something good is also born. Some of the *ninjutsu* students of the Hand and the shadow arts split away from their increasingly corrupt and power-hungry masters. They called themselves the Chaste, and vowed they would not be defiled by the ways of darkness, nor would they be tempted by the worldly treasures that had so driven their former brothers to greed and rapacity. Hidden in secret mountain retreats, they trained in the same mystical shadow arts and mastered the same deadly skills, but their goals were to balance out the dark influence of the Hand. And while it was never intended to be so—such things seldom are—a war began between the two factions.

Or maybe . . .

It was a game.

And so it raged. Through decade after decade, century after century, times of political riots, assassinations both successful and unsuccessful, and public violence. Unlike their dark-side counterparts, the Chaste couldn't offer wealth and power as rewards, so as they fought with the Hand, they began an endless quest for new warriors to fill the ranks of those they lost in battle, a never-ending search for the best of the best, for those among the people who were worthy of giving more than that which is expected of the everyday man or woman.

And as it is on the perfectly geometric playing field of the Go board, sometimes, for extraordinary game pieces, death is simply not enough. . . .

HELL'S KITCHEN, NEW YORK

Bob's head jerked as the ambulance bounced over yet other flaw in the street, a manhole cover or a bag of garbage or maybe, since it *was* New York, a pile of rags concealing a body lying in the middle of the road. "Crap," he said as he tried to hold onto his clipboard and fill in the report. "Ray, knock on the window and tell Pyle to slow down, would you? How fast he drives isn't going to make a difference anymore and I'd like to get to St. Luke's in one piece."

"Ditto," his younger partner muttered. He twisted on his seat and banged his fist twice on the Plexiglas separating the driver from the back part of the ambulance, then made a sawing motion across his neck when the third member of their team glanced in the mirror. He felt the momentum of the vehicle shift forward as it slowed suddenly and knew his buddy understood that there was no longer a reason to hurry. It was a shame, Ray thought again as his gaze cut to the woman. He couldn't help wondering what had happened, why she was dressed the way she was, and who had done the damage that had ultimately killed her. He'd pulled her hand back up next to her body and it was hard not to notice the black and yellow bruises covering her knuckles . . . oh, and let's not forget another puncture wound, this one going clean through her right hand.

Ray glanced at his partner, who was concentrating on filling out a form despite the movement of their vehicle. Ray's being senior on the job gave his older partner the thankless task of filling out the paperwork, a job Ray would have actually preferred to the option of cleaning up the bloodied bandages and now-empty syringes and used IV drips. Ray bent forward and let one knee drop to the rubber-covered floor; might as well gather up the used gauze and the paper wrappings from the—

11

Someone yanked open the back of the ambulance.

Both medics jerked around. There were two men standing there, each dressed completely in white. For a moment, what Ray was seeing didn't really register in his brain. The guys crouching outside were like ninjas, but not—they were almost like *negatives* of the black-clad warriors so often seen in film. Who'd ever heard of a ninja wearing white?

Before Ray could think about answering his own question, one of the white Ninjas leapt into the ambulance.

"Wait," Ray started to say. "We're the good guys, remember? Not the cops, not the—" His words choked off as the ninja held up a finger and wagged it back and forth, the universal *shhhh* motion. He wanted to keep talking but he didn't dare, then he forgot what he might have said anyway when the other ninja jumped gracefully into the back of the ambulance. Of all the things in the world that Ray could have imagined might happen, all he could do was sit there and watch in bewilderment as the white ninjas lifted the dead woman's body from the cart and slipped back out of the vehicle. One more

    slow

      motion

        blink

and they disappeared into the blackness of a New York midnight.

2

ELEKTRA.

She was floating, no, sleeping in blackness. No . . . that wasn't right either. She was . . . she was . . .

Nothing.

That was it, just nothing at all. No feeling, no dreaming, no emotion—

Elektra.

Something touched her.

No—that couldn't be right.

Go *away!*

She said it, she whispered it, she screamed it, but of course, there was no sound. She couldn't hear it; certainly whoever or *what*ever was trying to reach her couldn't. Why? Because she was gone, she wasn't alive, she wasn't *anything*. She was *dead*, even she somehow knew that. Nothing could reach her or hurt her, and that was good. No one—

But something definitely *was*.

Hands.

They were there, she *felt* them, even as she somehow realized that she had no right to, that her time upon the Earth was over and the material realm should have been forever out of her reach.

You are a warrior.

They touched her hands, her feet, her arms, legs, bringing sensation to the suddenly burning wounds in her stomach, palm and throat. They left trails of volcanic sensation across her forehead and the top of her skull and painted strips of agony around her elbows and knees, all pooling into a torturous, liquid fire spot just beneath her left breast—her heart.

Come back, Elektra.

Where before she'd had blessed nothingness, now she had a universe of torment, a timeless, endless pit of pain in which she was drowning. It soaked into every pore of her suddenly reawakening skin, burned the surface of her eyelids beneath her squeezed-shut lids, crept up her nose and filled her sinuses, mouth, and throat. She gagged and something—

Breathe!

—went down her throat and pushed its way into her windpipe. Maybe it was air, or energy, or a combination of both, but it felt like acid, like bleach, like a thousand different chemicals that were never meant to pass the lips of a human being. The well-toned muscles along her back and abdomen tightened, then twisted into full spasm mode, sending a stream of vicious white heat to radiate from the hole in her stomach along every single nerve ending until the torture found its way to all parts of her body.

Her eyelids squeezed together a final time, then flew open to see the first thing in the second part of her life.

Blue eyes, pale and sightless, gazed through her and into a realm she'd glimpsed but could now no longer see. They belonged to a stranger she had no way of knowing would soon become the focus of her second-chance existence.

Elektra fought to pull herself upright, then gagged as she leaned over the side of the low wooden pallet on which she had been placed. She hauled more air into her bruised lungs, and they hitched in protest, wanting to refuse it but not able to do so on their own. Another inhalation, another wretched, futile attempt at vomiting.

Finally, *finally*, Elektra was pulling in air in a semi-steady motion, although the effort cost her so much that all she could do was sit there with her head hanging so low that her long hair brushed the floor beneath the table on which she lay.

But the man at her side only smiled faintly as he stared into space and spoke to her in a soft, butter-smooth voice. "Only a warrior can come back from death," he said.

Later she would learn that the blind man's name was Stick, and he would be one of her teachers.

She would also discover that he'd forgotten to mention that even for a warrior, the second life is never quite like the first.

HIDDEN TRAINING CAMP

Before she'd died and come back, Elektra Natchios had trained with a number of sensei, and she had learned their crafts well. At the camp where she ended up after her stomach wound had finally closed and healed (mostly) and her body had regained its strength, she learned even more about the art of fighting. Additions to her fighting repertoire included the *bo*—long staff—eskrima sticks and the nunchaku, the whip and the kukri, along with the weapons and skills of dozens of other disciplines. Like the other students, Elektra pulled her hair back in a headband, dressed in white, and trained with others like herself—but not nearly as skilled—daily. She lived with them, ate with them, fought with them.

But she was never quite *one* of them, never a part of the subjective family existence and camaraderie that the others seemed to share simply by virtue of being there with each other. They were brothers and sisters because of proximity, the children of the emotionless sensei who ruled the camp and taught their arts with stern and unyielding methods. In their students the masters accepted no mistakes, no weaknesses, no slackers, and Elektra did not disappoint them. But they also condemned the American woman's need to shine, her hunger for competition and undying drive to be the best—they wanted her to be a soldier in their army, one small cog in the larger machine of their battle against darkness. But like the television commercials for the military, the ones she vaguely remembered from her previous life as the daughter of Nicholas Natchios, Elektra didn't want to be one part of an army.

She wanted to *be* the army.

There was so much anger inside her, for so many reasons—her mother, her father, Matt Murdock, the life that had been carved out of her existence and lost forever. She could feel her rage warring with the desire to do good. One second she would be practicing an *arnis* form with another student, each move perfectly in sync, both of them ostensibly learning the timing and the rhythm, the *perfection* of it. But then something inside her would take over and suddenly the student would be on the ground at her feet, or maybe his head would be caught in a figure-four combination made up of her left arm and right Kali stick. It was like someone else hearing her victim's choking sounds, feeling his heels drum uselessly against her shins as his air disappeared before his mind could formulate a way of escape.

A snap of realization, some small spark in her brain, would save her classmate at the last second. Many refused to pair with her, turning away to control their own fury as they reminded her tersely that they were in this camp to *learn*, not get hurt. Again and again the sensei reminded her that self-control was a part of that learning, a *necessary* part, and that she could never teach if she could not learn. Teach? She didn't care about teaching, and she was learning just fine. She had remarkable skills, moving with consummate skill and grace, incredible speed and strength. She was learning to be faster than her classmates, more brutal than her enemies, and better than her sensei.

And then her learning abruptly came to an end.

"I'll partner with you."

Elektra turned and studied the man who had spoken. He was taller than her, fit and muscular. His arms were toned and tight beneath the three-quarter length sleeves of his *gi*, the hair on his head shaven down to almost nothing. If she recalled correctly, his name was Patrick and he was having the same difficulty she was in finding sparring and training partners. He was an ex-Marine; rumor had it that he, too, had been brought back to life and he struggled with the same control issues—or lack of—that Elektra herself was said to have.

She grinned and stepped over to stand beside Patrick in line. Maybe she'd finally found a partner who was actually worthy of her efforts, someone who could take what she had to dish out in the pursuit of her own knowledge. The current lesson was in savate— French kickboxing—and they followed the routine the teacher dictated, weaponless sparring to hone techniques already learned, then choreographed practice to teach one another proper blocking and parrying. Expect the unexpected, they always said, and Patrick's hard punches and kicks only made Elektra grin and return them kind for kind. Then, with the toe of her shoe pointed in perfect savate fashion, she got bored with the repetitious *frontal* practice kick and aimed higher than the kicking shield Patrick was holding in front of his body. Her *frontal* kick caught him square in the hollow of his throat and he dropped, clawing at his neck as the useless leather shield dropped away.

The other students crowded around as the teacher ran to the fallen man. Staring down at him, Elektra felt no emotion other than triumph—and certainly no regret. As far as she was concerned, the fault was his. Had they not been told to expect the unexpected? Would a *real* opponent have been nice enough to aim his kick exactly where Patrick wanted it? He'd gotten what he deserved. Beyond that, despite what others had repeatedly said about her, she wasn't particularly angry . . . at least not at the moment.

After a long, tense moment, Patrick found his air and managed to stand. He glared at her, then turned his back and stalked away—she'd lost yet another training partner.

The sensei teaching the savate class turned to look at her. She could see the anger in his eyes and in the way the skin around his lips was so tight it had turned nearly white on his olive-colored face. He gestured at her, then dropped into a fighting stance, making the rest of the class members back nervously away from the pair.

Elektra only grinned.

The only protection they had were the padded boxing gloves, but that would have to be enough. She blocked and returned each of his punches, dancing nimbly out of reach as he aimed *fouettés* and *chassés*. This was fun, a game played with a partner who at least had the skill to challenge her, a little innocent recreation—

Then her sensei came in with a split-second *chassé latéral* kick that caught her across the back and knocked her to her knees.

Pain razored through her back and her belly, following the line of the internal scarring left by the *sai*—her own—that Bullseye had pushed all the way through her body. Her head fell forward and she gasped when she saw a spot of stunningly bright blood soak through the previously unmarred white of her *gi*—obviously her flesh still had a bit of healing to do. The pain faded almost instantly but her insides still throbbed, bringing back the horrendous memory of her final moments in that rooftop battle. The sting of the playing card edge that Bullseye had whipped across her throat had shocked her, but that had been nothing, *nothing*, compared to the all-consuming anguish as he'd impaled

Elektra using her own steel. Announced with all the enthusiasm of a circus hawker and undercut with Matt's faint cry of "Noooooooo!" Elektra would never forget the last words that Bullseye had said to her—

"And now, for my next trick!"

—right before he'd thrust her *sai* into her stomach, then twisted it so it came out her back. How confident he'd been as he threw her off the edge of the roof level on which they'd fought, then left her to die and gone off in search of other dark pursuits with which to entertain himself. If there was one thing Elektra had to be grateful for, it was that Bullseye's voice had *not* been the final one she would hear. She'd dragged herself up and forward until she and Matt had found each other, and it was in his loving arms that the light of her life had winked out.

Or so she'd thought.

Before she had been killed that night, Elektra had told Matt she would find him. No doubt he'd thought that promise fulfilled when she'd dragged her dying body over to him, but as far as she was concerned, that was a pledge that had yet to be fully consummated. And Matt Murdock—Daredevil—probably knew it, too—he was a smart man and she had great faith in his ability to read between the lines of Braille punched into the ankh she'd later left for him.

Today, however, Elektra needed to find someone else, someone deep inside her soul with the heart of a lion and

21

who would not tolerate being beaten again, no matter what the lesson to be learned, no matter who was teaching it. She would not be bested again, placed in danger again, humiliated again, even by her own martial arts instructors. She would not die. She would *not*.

Besides, this was *fun*.

She lifted her head and stared up at the sensei who'd kicked her, and she could feel her own eyes light up with the thrill of the hunt and the rage . . . and oh, there was so *much* of that. Could he see that in her? A part of her brain knew that the instructor standing in front of her was not the cause of her pain, at least not the mental part, and that in reality he would never intentionally hurt her. He was probably only trying to teach her a lesson, push upon her a bit of wisdom about self-control. But another part of her brain wanted no part of self-control. It desired only to fight, to retaliate and cause more pain than she had received and then to make it last that much *longer*. And that part was the stronger half, the overwhelming majority, and it *always* won.

While she had been on her knees, someone had tossed the sensei a *bo*, one of the master league ones made of hardened bamboo and covered with carvings. He held it at the ready, comfortable with its use and secure in his knowledge of the weapon's forms, especially when his opponent was down and clearly injured.

Even so, it didn't help him.

Elektra came up underneath it and when he swung

at her and twirled it end over end, she was already inside his circle of defense and spinning outward, seeing everything from his point of view. That made it easy to anticipate his next attack, and she disarmed him in seconds, striking back at him viciously, embarrassing him in front of the other students as they saw him defeated with his own weapon at the same time as he took a vicious double blow to his ribs and one leg. Now it was her instructor gasping on his knees before her, and there was a tickle—just that—at the back of her brain that hinted maybe she shouldn't have gone this far. But there was nothing to be done for it now, and so she let the bo slip from her fingers, turned her back, and walked away. That would teach him to be more careful about his lessons to her in the future.

She could feel the unfriendly gazes of her fellow students as she crossed the courtyard and headed to where Stick waited in the doorway of his modest cabin. Perhaps she should have been bothered by their displeasure, but she wasn't—she simply didn't care. There was no camaraderie for her here, no feeling of family or belonging. She had left her classmates behind almost immediately in the training, and when a student is superior to her teacher, it's very difficult to find friendship among her so-called peers. Since leaving Matt Murdock behind and losing her father, Elektra wasn't sure she could feel affection again, for anyone. Still, if she could find anything left in her being that resembled

23

affection, it would be for Stick, the enigmatic blind man she thought of as her rescuer from death.

Funny how someone not particularly tall or broadly built could radiate so much power, so much constrained grace and . . . *ability*. His age was a mystery to her, his calm face at odds with his snow white hair and the resilient way he trained and carried the trim body beneath the black gi. He stood straight and still, his slender right hand wrapped around a black staff. If eyes were, indeed, the windows to the soul, then the man must surely be soulless, because Elektra could see nothing in Stick's pale blue orbs but the reflection of herself. She saw that now, reading, somehow, the consequences of all that she had done in the last few minutes in a split-second of sightless eye contact, in the way his left hand gestured at her to join him.

Damn.

She stopped before him and bowed her head slightly in respect, even though he couldn't see the movement—he would know if she didn't, she was sure of it. "Sensei," she said. Suddenly she felt it all—the loneliness of being ostracized by her classmates, the anger in her own heart, even the shame felt by her instructor of being bested by a student. If only she would learn to think with her head instead of her heart, to weigh her choices before acting. Next time, she vowed silently, she would do just that. Next time, she—

"So what do you think?" Stick asked, breaking into her thoughts.

She inhaled. Perhaps, if she answered candidly, there would be no need for a next time. "I've got nothing more to learn here," she replied. "When do I get to do it for real?"

He didn't answer, just kept staring at her. Elektra couldn't help shifting uncomfortably. If this was how it felt to have him study her when he couldn't see, she didn't dare imagine what it might be like if he could.

Finally, he spoke. "Do you know the way, Elektra?"

She blinked in confusion, not sure how to answer or what response Stick was looking for—sometimes her teachers delved more into the philosophical than she was able to handle. Perhaps this was one of those times?

"*Kimagure,*" Stick continued when she stayed silent. "That is the way. The ability to control time, the future . . . even life and death."

Okay, this was even more out of her realm. "I don't understand," she admitted.

He nodded sagely, still gazing straight ahead. "No, you don't. And that is the problem."

Elektra frowned. "I know I'm the best student here."

Stick's expression turned regretful. "Not the best— the most *powerful*. You understand violence and pain, but you do not know the *way*."

Elektra stared at him as a chill rippled across the

back of her neck and crawled down her arms. Something here wasn't good. "Teach me, then."

As they always did, Stick's crystalline blue eyes stared straight ahead, making him impossible to read. "That is my point," he said. He sounded like a teacher explaining something for the tenth time to a student who just didn't get it. "I *can't* teach you." He paused. "I want you to go," he finally said.

She grinned with relief and stood up a little straighter. "On a mission? I agree, Sensei. Who do you want me to . . . uh, what do you do you want me to do?"

He waited to answer until Elektra started to become uncomfortable a second time. "Not a mission," he said softly. "Just . . . leave. Get out." He gave a curt nod that seemed more to support his own position than anything else. With his back ramrod straight and his light-colored eyes still focused on nothing she could see, Stick might as well have been made of ice. His next words confirmed his sudden coldness toward her.

She suddenly felt suffocated as she tried to fathom what he was saying. This couldn't be true, it *couldn't*. This camp—it was the only place she had now, the only place she belonged . . . or at least the closest she could come. To lose that on top of losing her father and Matt . . . it was *devastating*. What good was it to come back to life if the smallest of the things you gained by doing so was then taken away from you?

Her hands twisted together hard, bruising her fingers, then she scrubbed at her face like someone trying to wake up from a bad dream. Finally, she looked at him again. Her mouth worked, but shock made it difficult for her to speak. "But, Sensei . . . I have no place to go. Is . . . is this a test?" Her voice was small, uncertain.

"No, it's *not* a test." Stick's voice was harsher than she had ever heard it. "Now *go!*"

So with her soul swelled with rage, Elektra turned her back on her sensei and stalked out of the compound, determined to leave it behind forever.

3

A SECLUDED MOUNTAIN SKI LODGE
IN SWITZERLAND

IN SOMEONE ELSE'S LIFE, THIS WOULD HAVE BEEN A picture-perfect evening.

But as he swirled the fragrant, dark amber liquid in his glass, DeMarco could think of only the one thing in his life that made perfection impossible:

Fear.

The exquisite, snow-covered mountains that overlooked this multimillion-dollar vacation home were like implacable witnesses to the terror that was boiling inside him. DeMarco had the best of everything—this house, with its twenty-four rooms filled with the most tasteful of everything—a Rolls-Royce, a Mercedes, a Hummer, and three other SUVs in the garage, a closet full of designer clothes so handsome that most movie stars would drool over them. Even the scotch in his crystal glass was sixty-year-old Macallan, the rarest and most expensive in the world, a treat for the richest of the rich, something in which even he rarely indulged.

Of course, if he was going to die tonight, he might as well drink the stuff, the whole damned bottle. It wasn't as if he was going to get another opportunity.

DeMarco stared at the fire burning cheerfully in the stone fireplace, then let his gaze wander around the room. Did they have scotch in the afterlife? *Was* there an afterlife? He'd had a good run on this earth, so he didn't have much to complain about there. Perhaps he should have taken pains to take it with him, like the ancient Egyptians. Even before he'd come into money, back when he was a very young man, his piercing blue eyes and slender good looks had made him a legendary playboy with the ladies, and they certainly hadn't hurt him when he'd proposed to his first wife. She had been a millionairess who met an unfortunate end in a skiing "accident" only two years after their wedding on the slopes of a mountain much like this one (which actually had belonged to his *second* wife, Beverly, whom he laughingly referred to in conversation as *one of my former wives*).

Becoming a widower had given him the capital to get started and, of course, the marriage itself had launched him into the appropriately moneyed circles; from there, he had taken only a few short and brutal stepping-stones until guaranteeing himself a slot at the very top of the money web. And if he hadn't been such a . . . *nice* person along the way, then so be it. He'd like to meet the person who could honestly say he'd gained his billions—yes, *billions*—by being "nice."

And therein was his trade-off.

DeMarco took a drink of Macallan and couldn't help wondering how long he would have lived had he chosen a different path in life. What if he and Claudette, that nearly forgotten first wife, had actually gotten along, and what if she hadn't threatened to leave him if he cheated on her again? In fact, if he was *really* going to go the morality route, what if he *hadn't* done exactly that—cheated on her and gotten caught? Claudette might still be alive, they might even have had a couple of children—ones who actually liked him—and done the whole happily-ever-after thing.

Nah. That just wasn't him.

"How much longer do I have? Minutes? Hours?"

DeMarco hadn't realized he'd spoken aloud until the head of his security force, a middle-aged man named Warren Bauer, answered him from where he was stationed at a bank of security monitors. The bright green screens showed armed personnel in all the key places around the estate, and all were fit, alert, and ready for trouble. There were no slackers on Bauer's crew. "You're gonna be fine, Mr. DeMarco."

DeMarco glanced over at him and frowned slightly. Bauer was a nice enough–looking guy who took his job very seriously. He even dressed the part, sporting a crewcut above a heavy-duty flak jacket and double holsters crisscrossing his chest, with each side holding a no-screwing-around Llama 9mm Omni. He didn't know what they were loaded with—he'd always had the money to leave the unpleasant things like that to paid employees—but with circumstances being what they were, DeMarco was sure Bauer had gone for something particularly nasty.

Bauer adjusted the state-of-the-art headset pushed into his ear. "Perimeter, what's your status?" There was only a one- or two-second delay before the security man received a half dozen crackling reassuring replies. With a slightly self-satisfied smile, Bauer settled back on his stool, then turned to study DeMarco. "You're gonna be fine," he repeated. "Just go easy on the sauce, sir." The way Bauer raised his eyebrow made his boss wonder if he really believed there was going to be a problem at all. Some people, no matter how smart, could be spectacular fools. He himself knew about that. "In case we have to move you," Bauer added.

DeMarco almost chuckled. Instead of obeying, he lifted the glass and took a long, exaggerated sip of the buttery smooth scotch. He rolled the liquid over his tongue, wishing he could appreciate it, then swallowed. "Why bother?" he grated. "You can't stop her. Nobody can stop her."

Bauer sat up a little straighter, all ears. Until now, his

wealthy boss hadn't said a word about why they were here, other than he was afraid he'd become the target of an assassination assignment. Bauer had assumed a corporate hit attempt, probably a couple of well-trained ex-soldiers turned mercenaries like himself. Now Mr. DeMarco's words opened up a whole new arena of interesting possibilities. "Her?"

DeMarco ground his teeth and stared at his glass for a long moment. What the hell—it was well past confession time. He'd done so many things wrong in his life that he ought to be able to own up on his last night. "I didn't tell you," he admitted. "I was afraid you wouldn't take the job." He paused, then ran his fingers through his carefully styled hair, leaving it shaggy and out of place. He didn't care. Bauer almost didn't catch the rich man's next mumbled words. "I never should have hired you."

But Bauer was more interested than afraid. He'd taken a chance with DeMarco—under normal circumstances, he would have never hired on in an information vacuum, but DeMarco was paying damned well. It looked like now he was finally going to get the goods he'd wanted since signing on to this gig a week ago. "Who do you think's after you?"

DeMarco took so long to answer that Bauer almost gave up. It wouldn't have been the first time the guy had stonewalled him, and he'd learned a long time ago that there are certain times when you just couldn't push rich men. But finally . . .

"I'm told her name is Elektra."

Bauer's mouth fell open, then it was all he could do not to bust out laughing. The most he would allow himself was a condescending smile. "She's an urban legend, sir. That woman died years ago."

DeMarco cleared his throat, then polished off the last of the Macallan and set his glass aside. "Yeah," he said. "That's what I thought. Until last month." With DeMarco studying his hands and Bauer studying DeMarco, neither noticed something move on one of the monitors, a sort of *flash* moving too fast for the eye to follow, the glimpse of something long and red before it was yanked out of sight.

Bauer had heard stories about this Elektra woman, sure—you couldn't run a high-dollar security business like his without hearing the tales. He still believed they were nothing but urban legends, probably something started on the Internet that had spiraled into the realm of uncontrollability. The guy with the flat tire and the trunk full of torture tools at Wal-Mart, the five-dollar bill being returned by the honest serial killer, the missing child one whose place of origin changed as often as the moon went into a new cycle, and, of course, the incredible Iraq camel spider photo. Still, Bauer found himself listening to DeMarco in spite of himself, in spite of the fact that he knew this couldn't possibly be true. If he had to justify his attentiveness, he'd have to say it was because of the older man's fear—DeMarco was so saturated with it that Bauer could practically *smell* it on him. He could certainly see it in DeMarco's body language, in the way he went from staring at his own hands to gripping the arms of his chair so firmly that his knuckles were white. DeMarco's vivid blue eyes were bloodshot, testament not to drinking but to the sleepless nights of the last week or so, and his gaze kept darting around the room as if he expected someone, or *something*, to simply materialize in front of his eyes at any moment.

DeMarco hauled himself out of his chair and went to the antique sideboard. Ignoring Bauer's earlier warning, he plucked a clean crystal glass from the silver tray in the center of the sideboard, then snatched up the bottle of Macallan next to it. DeMarco's hand was shaking badly and Bauer's pulse jumped when his boss nearly lost his grip on the bottle of sixty-year-old scotch, but the other man caught himself and sloshed a more than generous amount into his glass. He turned and held it toward Bauer invitingly, but Bauer just shook his head. Tempting—when would he ever have the chance to taste scotch like this again?—but saying yes in situations like this had a way of coming back to bite you in the rear end.

DeMarco made his way unsteadily back to his seat,

but Bauer didn't think DeMarco's legs were shaking because he was drunk. "When you've lived the life I have," DeMarco said as he settled back onto the Italian leather, "you make enemies. My private security detail were ex–Secret Service." He nodded to himself. "The best money could buy." He lifted the glass to his face and inhaled, savoring the rich scent of the scotch. "She killed nine of them and crippled two others," he said flatly. "All of it in less than half an hour. I barely got out of the building." He paused and tilted his head contemplatively. "In fact, it felt like she *let* me go."

Bauer's eyes narrowed as he took in the information. An impressive tale, but was it really the Elektra of modern legend? Maybe, but it sounded more like the work of a highly trained team than one person.

DeMarco inhaled, then tilted his glass and let a generous part of the liquor slide down his throat. "She found me two days later," he said in a raspy voice. "In Monte Carlo. And she let me go *again*. I escaped by helicopter to Monsanto's estate." He squinted at Bauer. "You've worked for Mr. Monsanto, haven't you?"

Bauer nodded. "A couple of times."

A corner of DeMarco's mouth pulled up in an unpleasant grimace. "He won't be needing you anymore," he told his security man. "He's dead, along with a good chunk of his private army."

Bauer jerked, unable to mask his surprise. Monsanto and the best of his security crew were dead? Monsanto's private "army," as DeMarco had put it, was almost as legendary as this fictional Elektra. The couple of times he'd pulled duty for the Japanese tycoon had only been on special occasions when Monsanto had needed to fatten up the ranks, such as during his daughter's wedding. Even then Bauer and his men had been relegated to the most menial of assignments, such as patrolling the parked vehicles, while Monsanto's own men had carried out their usual hawk-eyed supervision of the sensitive areas.

"So," DeMarco continued, "I'm here. No one else would have me. Thanks to her, this is as far as I'm going."

The screen at the far right on the bank of monitors behind Bauer flickered, but neither man noticed as a hand reached into view and plucked the headset from the body of a downed guard. A second later the guard's limp body was dragged offscreen, leaving nothing visible but his empty post.

DeMarco gestured to the impressive room around him. "You know what's funny? I forgot I owned this place. It was a ski chalet for my second wife—I always had a fondness for skiing—and a good place to store liquor."

Bauer stared at DeMarco, feeling his own features work their way into a frown. In spite of his disbelief, DeMarco's story was getting to him, working its way into his head and starting that damnable tickle of doubt. That was bad—a man in his position not only needed to show confidence, he needed to *be* confident, absolutely sure of himself and that his men could handle anything that might be thrown at them. He couldn't let himself start to think that just one woman might be able to undermine all that. DeMarco's next words didn't help.

The rich man leaned forward. "Listen, Bauer, why don't you . . . ?" DeMarco's voice faded for a moment and he swallowed, as if he had to force himself to say the words. "Why don't you take your men and go." It was a statement rather than a question. "Save yourselves."

Bauer blinked, then set his jaw. He'd be damned if some feminine fairy tale was going to run him or his men off the job, especially when there wasn't anything supporting the story past one semidrunk billionaire. Forget it. "Relax, Mr. DeMarco," he said with a joviality he didn't really feel. "I don't know about those other guys, but we're going to protect you until you—"

An alarm sounded on one of the monitors behind him.

Bauer whirled and stalked back to the console, then flipped a set of switches below a monitor that was showing nothing but an empty stretch of landscaping at the outside southeast corner of the estate. "How's it going out there on the perimeter?" he asked crisply. He glanced at the other screens and scowled when he realized that he couldn't see any of his men. It seemed his team of bad-ass professionals had virtually vanished. His voice sharpened. "Delta, what's your status?" he demanded.

Nothing.

Before he could ask again, Bauer jerked as the computer monitors began blanking out, one by one. Within three seconds, all that was left was a nearly complete line of downed screens. They looked like black, oversized ghostly eyes staring at him.

"The better the assassin," DeMarco said softly, "the closer he—or she—can get before you even know they're there."

Only the last one still showed a man on patrol at the front door, and even as Bauer grabbed for the switch to warn him over the intercom, the guy—his best one—was jerked out of view. An instant later that screen went as dark as the others, and a split second after that, Bauer gasped as he heard a gunshot.

"Alpha team!" Bauer's voice rose to a shout into his headphones. "Bravo, *report!*"

DeMarco's voice came from behind him as the man spoke around the lip of his glass of scotch. "They say Elektra whispers in your ear before she kills you."

Bauer resisted the urge to snarl at his boss as he heard more gunfire echo from somewhere else in the ski lodge, then shouts and screams—those were his men out there being hurt, maybe even dying. Before he could decide what to do next, the monitors suddenly flickered back to life . . . but all they showed was static.

With his lips drawn back into a slash of fury, Bauer pulled one of his guns free, then the other one.

"Do you have children, Bauer?" DeMarco asked.

Before Bauer could answer, the lights went out.

For an unnerving three seconds, there was nothing but darkness and the harsh sound of the two men's panicked breathing. Then there was an industrial-sounding hum and a clank, and the formerly warm sitting room was bathed in the cold, blue light of the backup battery-generated lamps.

Bauer eyed the door to the room, then flicked his gaze nervously toward the overabundance of windows. "Children?" he replied dutifully. "Yes, sir. Two girls, eight and five. What about you?"

DeMarco shrugged as if he didn't have a problem in the world and this was a time for nothing more than idle conversation. "None who still talk to me." He paused, then wobbled to his feet and once again headed for the sideboard and his scotch. "Listen, go home to them, Bauer. I don't want any more orphans on my account."

Bauer turned and gaped at him, not believing that the guy was just walking nonchalantly in front of all that glass. Was he *inviting* a gunshot? "No offense, sir, but could you just shut up and stay *down?*"

DeMarco didn't answer . . . but someone else did, whispering silkily over the earpiece of Bauer's headset.

"Listen to your boss, Bauer. Go home to your family."

"Christ!" Bauer cried and instinctively ripped off the headset and threw it aside.

DeMarco looked up from the task of pouring himself another outrageously expensive glass of scotch. He nodded, almost in approval. "She likes messing with your head." He made his way gingerly back to his chair, sat, then reached over to the end table and picked up a folded newspaper. As if there were nothing else in the world to worry about, he unfolded it on his lap and stared at the front page.

Bauer turned away, not letting himself get sidetracked by Bauer's strange sense of acceptance. Nearly crouching, he cat-walked halfway across the room and leveled his gun on the door, the only way into the room. For a long moment there was nothing but silence, inside the room and out. Then—

Creeeeeak.

With his expression pulled into a snarl, Bauer unloaded the full thirteen shots of first one Llama, then the other, all over the surface of the door. The gunshots were nearly deafening, and they left his ears ringing and his vision full of blue flashes of light; after that, anything on the other side couldn't be anything but Swiss cheese. That the entrance was still upright was a testament to the thickness of the fancy hardwood door; his eyes were quickly recovering from the muzzle flashes, but gun smoke was still clogging Bauer's vision;

40

even so, there was no doubt that the surface of the extra-wide door was covered with smoking holes. Bauer wasn't taking any chances; as he moved toward what was left of it, he was already dropping out both spent clips and slamming new ones into place.

In one spot, several bullet holes had made an opening large enough for the security man to see light through, that same bluish glow of backup lights in the hallway. Nothing was evident there, so he cautiously pushed the door open. With every sense on high alert, Bauer leaned out and glanced first left, then right—again, nothing. With two full clips at the ready and nothing in the hallway, he felt pretty confident as he turned back to address DeMarco.

Something sharp and cold stung as it pressed ever so lightly against the prickling flesh on the back of his neck.

"You can't fight a ghost, Bauer."

The security manager swallowed when he heard the feminine voice. Was this really the fabled Elektra? He wondered where the hell she'd been hiding and how she knew his name—now that he thought about it, this was the second time she'd used it. Had she been within earshot this entire time, reveling in DeMarco's fear and laughing at Bauer's own misplaced self-confidence?

The point of whatever was digging into his skin pressed harder, and it didn't take a genius to know she wanted him to put down his guns. There was a decorative table to each side of the entrance door, and he carefully set down both Llamas, directing the barrels toward the wall—if he got the chance to grab at them, he didn't want to idiotically shoot himself. As he gave the weapons a little push away from his body, he felt the metal ease away from his neck. A little more, and—

Bauer spun, chambering his right leg close to his body and bringing it up in a high spinning crescent kick.

There was nothing behind him but empty air.

He hissed as his foot reached the apex of his kick, then he felt a hand grab his ankle and yank straight up. His body went airborne as his other leg followed the momentum of the first, and Bauer had just a moment to glimpse red—some kind of costume—before he crashed back to the floor and sank into darkness.

DeMarco watched the whole scene play out without moving, or running, or even wincing. Maybe he was too terrified to move, or maybe he was past the point of caring, numb and surrendering like a baby antelope that goes limp as it feels the jaws of a lioness close around its neck. As the woman sent to kill him moved smoothly across the room, DeMarco let his gaze drop to his glass. He didn't want to look into her eyes, not yet—God knows what he would see there. And yes, there was still a little Macallan left in his glass. Good. A man shouldn't have to die without a decent drink in his hand.

DeMarco could just make out Elektra's distorted, ghostly reflection in the side of the crystal. "So," he said softly. "Here we are at last." She didn't respond, so he kept talking. "That red outfit—I love it. And the knives, very fancy. What do you call them?" She still didn't answer and this time he risked a glance in her direction. She was just standing there, staring at him.

"It must be hard," he said thoughtfully. "Sneaking up on people dressed like that. How do you do it?" De-Marco realized his hand was aching; when he looked down, he saw that he was gripping the cut glass so hard that the edges of his fingernails had turned purple. He was also vaguely aware that he was babbling, his words tumbling out and revealing how afraid he was. Even so, he couldn't stop. It didn't matter anyway. "So what happens now?" he finally found the courage to ask. "You just kill me straight out or what?"

He waited, but there was still nothing but silence. Strangely, he was all out of questions and comments, didn't have a clue what to say next although he still felt somehow obligated to talk.

"Don't worry," Elektra said suddenly. "Death's not that bad."

Her placid, low voice came from behind his chair and DeMarco barely stopped himself from turning to look at her. When had she gone around behind him? But he wasn't ready to really face her, not yet. In spite of the scotch, his mouth was dry; he rubbed the back of one hand raggedly across his lips. "How do you know?" he rasped.

Her voice was so low he almost didn't hear her answer. "I died once."

DeMarco's eyes widened but he stayed motionless in his chair. So the rumors were true—Elektra *had* been killed. Not a near-death experience as some claimed, but an *actual* death event. He couldn't help his curiosity. "What was it like? Floating out of your body into a white light and all that crap?" He stopped and licked his cracking lips, wondering if his language had offended her, wondering if it was the thing that would trigger her into action. "Uh . . . sorry." He took a deep breath. "By the way, this scotch is like two hundred bucks a swallow. Have some when you're done. I'd hate it to go to waste when—"

DeMarco never had the opportunity to finish his sentence.

He'd been so sure that his babbling was successful, that Elektra had no idea about the gun he had hidden on his lap the whole time, the one he'd tucked into the folded newspaper this morning and about which even Bauer hadn't had a clue. It was a fine piece, a small but deadly Heckler & Koch P9S .45 double action. How foolish of him to ever believe he'd be able to so much as squeeze the trigger, much less move on his chair and actually try to aim. One of Elektra's deadly swords—he still hadn't a clue what they were really called—hit him with so much force that it went through his chest and pierced the back of his chair . . . *after* its blade threaded through the trigger so that he wouldn't have been able to use the weapon anyway.

But of course, DeMarco was dead well before he could realize any of that.

Elektra stared down at the dead man. DeMarco's eyes were open, his gaze fixed on her but seeing nothing. Before now she'd seen him only in photographs and hadn't realized that his eyes were such a spectacular shade of bright, ocean blue . . . very much like someone from far out of her past. She wished they'd closed so that she didn't have to look at them, didn't have to wonder if he had children who'd inherited that same eye color or who had taken after whatever wife he'd been married to at the time of their birth. She didn't want to think of him as a man, as a *person*, even someone deserving of his fate—he was just a target, something impersonal and meaningless, an ant under the foot of that giant called fate.

Elektra pulled out the sai stuck in his chest using a clean, fluid movement, then picked up the linen napkin next to DeMarco's glass of scotch and used it to slowly wipe the blade clean. Now that the house was quiet and all the guards were taken care of, she felt almost melancholy, although she wasn't sure whether it was because she had completed her work or because she'd killed not only DeMarco but at least three of the half dozen guards around the external perimeter.

She couldn't stop herself from glancing over to where Bauer lay unmoving on the carpet. Was he dead? Probably. Elektra wasn't absolutely sure, but she also wasn't going to check—it wasn't part of her employment to play good Samaritan, and that was a fool's task when she herself had been the one to put these men down in the first place. Even so, she couldn't help remembering when Bauer had answered DeMarco's question and she had been listening in—

"Do you have children, Bauer?"

"Children? Yes, sir. Two girls, eight and five . . ."

There was a certain phrase she used to remind herself about what she was doing and who she was, her place in the scheme of the world and the life she had chosen to live. She muttered it now—

"It's just a job."

—and again as she stepped over Bauer's silent, bleeding form and slipped out of the room—

"It's just a *job*."

—and she kept saying it to herself long into the longer night that followed.

4

TOKYO, JAPAN

At times like these, Roshi found peace among the stunning colors in his orchid garden.

Caring for the flowers gave the master time to think and analyze, meditate and work on those problems that troubled him most. There was, usually, nothing here but the silence of nature, although nature could never be called truly silent—at least a half dozen different birds sang from every direction, the insects clicked and buzzed, the bees hummed around the inviting, bright-colored blossoms. It was therapeutic to sit here on the polished teak bench, dressed in a traditional plain Japanese robe and clogs, while the wind sang around him, quite restful to the mind, body, and soul. He also enjoyed hand-trimming the orchid nubs with his fingertips, imparting his appreciation of their timeless beauty with every small movement he offered that aided in their care.

But even the wisest of men will tell you that serenity is always short-lived.

He looked up when he caught a tiny movement out of the corner of his eye. One of his servants stood about six feet away, hands folded patiently in front of his black uniform as he waited to be noticed. At Roshi's small nod of acknowledgment, the man bowed his head respectfully and spoke quietly. "Master Roshi, they have arrived."

Another nod and the servant left him, and although outwardly Roshi made no sign, inwardly he felt a tickle of tension as he got slowly to his feet. He hated to leave the sanctity of the orchid garden behind, wished it were situated somewhere far away, perhaps in the clear country air of Naoshima Island, or on the farther outskirts of Fukuoka City—there he could enjoy the amenities of civilization but still have a sense of being far away from it. But it was not his destiny to be a farmer, or a gardener; rather, he was what he was—one of the key members of the Hand . . . really an aging Japanese man who occasionally escaped reality in his tiny garden on the top of a skyscraper in the affluent part of the Greater Tokyo Area. But there was little peace to be found in an area with more than thirty-three million people.

Roshi did not hurry. In his private quarters, he shed his robe and washed his face and hands carefully before finally joining his waiting visitors in the opulent board and conference room. One, Meizumi, was a middle-aged business acquaintance, steady and conscientious—a thinker. But the other, Kirigi, was an impatient youngster, impetuous despite his traditional garb, and Roshi felt a strange mixture of sadness and regret when he looked at him. In his time, the youth of Japan had been more respectful, had been raised on a diet of patience and discipline. Now this newest generation was very much like the *anime* characters they seemed to adore—fast-moving, disobedient, and violent.

They waited—Kirigi with jittery, twitching limbs that revealed his inherent restlessness—while Roshi carefully positioned himself at the head of the table. While Meizumi was seated to Roshi's right, Kirigi, the younger and more dangerous of the two, stood by the door. He seemed both stiff and relaxed at the same time, an intriguing combination. His energy and enthusiasm showed in the hint of a smile at one corner of his mouth, a true indicator of his immaturity. An experienced man would have known to keep his face expressionless when greeting his elders.

Roshi pressed his lips together and regarded the two younger men. "The treasure continues to elude us."

Kirigi lifted one eyebrow, clearly interested in this thinly disguised opportunity. "Yes," he said simply.

Outraged, Meizumi gaped at Kirigi, then propelled himself to his feet.

Kirigi ignored him. "Perhaps if we had pursued it sooner . . . and more aggressively." He let his words trail off.

Now Meizumi was clearly furious. "You *dare* to blame Roshi?"

He balled his fists, but Roshi only smiled. A glance froze Meizumi where he stood. "Our methods seem too mild for Kirigi," Roshi commented.

A less astute man would have missed it, but Roshi caught the faintest of expressions that made it clear that was exactly what Kirigi thought. Even so, Kirigi opted for a more diplomatic response and he bowed his head to acknowledge the experience of the older man. "Not at all, Sensei. But if we cannot have the weapon ourselves, allow me to make sure it does not fall into the hands of others who might use it against us."

Meizumi also bowed his head, even as he shot a venomous look in Kirigi's direction. "Master, allow me to do this. Things of this nature must be handled smoothly. *Quietly.*"

Kirigi glanced at Meizumi and smirked slightly, but said nothing, even when Roshi's next words sliced into his pride.

"Then work smoothly, Meizumi. And quickly."

Meizumi bowed again to Roshi, then turned and did the same to Kirigi. The sneer on his face clearly said he was savoring his victory, but it faltered at the unconcerned look on Kirigi's calm features. When Kirigi bowed deeply to him and Roshi, then withdrew without protest, Meizumi wondered darkly if this wasn't exactly what Kirigi had wanted.

Kirigi strode out of the conference room with his head held arrogantly high, leaving Meizumi to glower after him. Did Roshi really believe that fool was up to the task of getting the treasure? Kirigi had seen through his *kimagure* that Elektra was involved, and the woman was as much a legend in her homeland as he was in his. Because of this, Roshi and his ignorant assistant would soon find out that it would take much more than the skills of an ordinary—or even an extraordinary—ninja to accomplish what he wanted here.

He, on the other hand, would not underestimate the assassin so easily. Kirigi had only to look to his own stable of killers to know just how deadly a woman could be, how potentially devastating her power. While it was true that heroes and antiheros grew large in the minds of the common man—Japanese folklore had his own slender frame described as that of a seven-foot-tall giant weighing in at three hundred pounds—it took only a fraction of the truth to annihilate an enemy. To his own arsenal Kirigi could add his mystical knowledge and self-healing properties, and Elektra had her endless knowledge of the shadow arts and the ways of war, plus her incredible athleticism. Really, what tools of war, *true* war, could the hapless Meizumi bring to the field in the battle that was about to take place? Kirigi's arsenal, on the other hand, was varied, rich in weapons, steeped in dark mysticism.

Yes, time would show Master Roshi that Meizumi was little beyond an ill-chosen warrior. And for that— Repercussions.

There always were.

AN UNKNOWN LOCATION

There was nothing to hold Elektra to this place.

She'd lived in dozens just like it—or maybe they had all been different. She couldn't remember, she didn't care. They were just . . . boxes, big containers to hold the temporary items that made whatever temporary life she'd set up there temporarily more comfortable. Standing just inside the front entrance and staring around the living room, Elektra could feel nothing but exhaustion, complete and all-encompassing, almost overpowering. She closed her eyes for a moment and felt the sensation sweep over her, then her eyelids snapped open. No, she would *not* let her life beat her. She had chosen her path, and *she* was the one in control of it, not the other way around. Starting over again might make her feel tired, but at least that was better than sadness.

She made herself stand straighter, then purposefully marched into the kitchen and yanked open the silverware drawer, pulling until the entire thing came free of the cabinet. She upended it into the sink, barely noticing the horrendous *crash* as the metal hit the porcelain.

She slid the empty drawer back into place, then bent and snagged a bottle of liquid bleach from beneath the sink, the kind that supposedly smelled like flowers. She wrinkled her nose as she unscrewed the top and poured it over the sink's contents. Flowers? Not likely.

With that done, she did the same to the drawer holding the larger cooking utensils. Elektra's eyes watered as she repeated the routine and doubled the amount of bleach in the deep sink. She'd have to do the dishes next, stack them into the dishwasher and run it with the bleach instead of detergent. There was so much to do—vacuum the carpets, mattress, furniture, then empty the vacuum cleaner itself and take the filled bag somewhere else to be thrown out, get rid of the laundry and any clothes—which meant most of them—that she couldn't readily carry. While she preferred modern and tasteful furniture and apartments, she also tried to keep her living space clean and sparse and free of clutter. Very few statues, no photographs at all, and only the most necessary paintings or framed posters, all nameless things she could easily leave behind. Elektra certainly didn't allow herself to collect knickknacks and things of which she might grow fond—when she had to move, she had to go fast and she didn't need baggage, emotional *or* material, to bog her down.

The master bathroom was next—she'd never used the second one—and in there she swept all but a few select items out of her medicine cabinet and vanity into a garbage bag for disposal. Then the most personal of her living spaces, the bedroom itself, and the one area where she allowed herself to relax a little and enjoy her quiet time. But now? So much for all the expensive, handmade clothes and couture that dotted the dresser's top, the silk scarves that hung over the footboard of the bed, the small cut glass bowl of potpourri and scented candles—all of it went into yet another three of the heavy, oversized garbage bags.

With the last of the expendables bagged up, Elektra went back into the kitchen and started working on the floor, down on her knees like a washerwoman armed with a spray bottle of 409 and a couple of rags. She was halfway finished when she heard the knock on the door; she ignored it and kept working, letting her arm muscles move into a rhythm that, while not soothing, kept her body busy and gave her mind something truly benign on which to focus.

Her caller didn't bother to knock a second time, just opened the door and stepped into the apartment. She could see the front hallway from her position, and she barely glanced up at the man who walked in. As usual, McCabe was wearing an impeccable black cashmere Kingston overcoat that moved with his body as if it were sewn into place; in one hand was a cognac-colored leather Vachetta duffle bag, in the other, a quilted Prada shoulder bag with chain and leather straps. He was a handsome, youngish looking man of maybe thirty-five, with light brown hair and a flawlessly clean shaven face. She had to acknowledge that he had exquisite taste.

He looked down at her, his face expressionless. "You think that's safe? Leaving your door unlocked?"

Elektra didn't bother to answer, just kept scrubbing at the floor. He stepped into the room and leaned over, but before he could set the duffle bag on the floor, she lifted her head. "No—stop, McCabe. Don't put it down. I already cleaned there."

McCabe shrugged, then stepped backward and set the duffle and Prada bag by the front door. He watched her for a few moments without saying anything before he finally asked the question she knew was coming. "Why do you always do this?"

Elektra had given him the same answer at least a dozen times before, but words, at least these, were free. "To get rid of my DNA."

As he always did, McCabe only laughed and shook his head. He nodded toward the duffle, and Elektra took a final swipe at the floor, then rose and went over to unzip it. As she expected, it was filled with blocks of one hundred dollar bills encircled by rubber bands. "I just picked it up," he told her. "I know you like to look at it."

She let that go by her, staring at the money with dull eyes. Maybe once it had meant something, but not anymore. Now it wasn't much more than just green and white paper. "It's all there?" she asked, because she knew he thought she should.

He nodded. "Less my ten percent."

The agent's commission, of course. Funny how you could broker a killing just like a real estate deal. Three or four bedrooms, and hey, would you like a decapitation with that? Sighing, she hefted the duffle bag out of habit, testing its weight before letting it drop back to the floor. "Half to Barbados," she began.

"And half to the bank on the Isle of Man," he finished for her. "You know, you can do a lot better in mutual funds. My brother's got this great—"

"No, thanks."

If he was insulted, McCabe gave no indication of it. When she started pulling together the remnants of her cleaning job, he tugged out the earphones he was wearing—she was never quite sure if they were for music or communication—and regarded her with a more serious expression. "You racked up quite the body count on this one, Elektra," he said pointedly. "We were only getting paid for DeMarco."

She didn't look up from her chores. "It had to be done."

"Did it?"

Now she scowled and did look up, ready for an argument, albeit one in which she wasn't sure how she'd defend her position. But McCabe only regarded her dispassionately and held his tongue, so she inhaled and let it go as she got together the rest of the cleaning bottles and the dirty rags and stuffed them into the last open garbage bag. "Anyway," she finally added, "it spreads the legend. Ups the price."

"Always important," McCabe conceded. He cracked his knuckles. "Speaking of which, we got a new offer."

"Let's skip this one," Elektra said a little too quickly. "I need a breather." His eyebrows lifted in surprise, but he said nothing. His silence was unnerving and made her feel compelled to continue. "I'm . . . tired."

McCabe regarded her carefully, his green eyes bright and penetrating. Sometimes he could make her feel like an interesting insect beneath the lens of a microscope. "You getting any sleep?" She shrugged, not saying either way, but he wasn't finished with his interrogation. "You try those Chinese herbs I gave you?"

He couldn't see it, but Elektra only rolled her eyes as she grabbed two more of the filled garbage bags and dragged them toward the door.

He correctly took her silence to mean no. "You're going to crash, baby," he told her pointedly. "You *know* that."

What could she say? She didn't sleep; she seldom

ate; she worked out obsessively. This was her life, and what she had made of it. For some reason it seemed impossible to change. Maybe if she took some time off—

"You ever get laid?" he demanded suddenly.

That stopped her, and she turned and gave him a murderous it's-none-of-your-business glare. He threw up his hands in mock surrender, then finally started helping her with the garbage bags. After a few moments, he murmured, "It's a lot of money—the new offer."

Elektra pressed her lips together in irritation. She hated being pushed. "Look, McCabe—"

"All right," he said, cutting her off. "Take some time off, then. Call me when you want to work."

She blinked as he dropped the last of the bags with the others, then grabbed up the Vachetta duffle and headed for the door. She could use some time off, she knew that, but . . .

What would she do if she got it?

Suddenly she thought of days, weeks, maybe even a month or two stretching out in front of her, all that time with nothing to do and no one with whom she could fill the emptiness, nothing on which to focus all of her . . . *energy*. It would be just like now . . . no, *worse* than now.

"How much?" she asked suddenly. For some reason, she just had to know, even though at the same time it made her angry at herself for asking. "Just tell me that."

58

One side of McCabe's mouth lifted in a satisfied smile and he let the duffle bag drop to the floor so he could hold up two fingers. She stared at him, torn between the unheard-of amount of assassination money and the need to just get away from the dirty work that had become her existence.

"I could give it to someone else," he said, but she could see the faint smirk still pulling up one side of his mouth.

"They wouldn't pay that to someone else," she said in a tired voice. It was a not-so-gentle statement about a dark fact that McCabe surely already knew. After all, hadn't she been the one talking about spreading the legend and getting her price to go up?

McCabe's mouth stretched into a knowing smile. "They did ask specifically for you."

She bowed her head, already surrendering. McCabe knew it, too—before she could change her mind, he grabbed the duffle again and headed for the door. "The location's in there," he said, jerking his head toward the Prada bag. "I'll call you when I get the target."

There was no one in the basement this late at night, although she was always taking a chance when she went through her closing routine. Sometimes Fridays brought the oddest people into the laundry room, everything from battered housewives to semihigh Goths doing once-a-month laundry before hitting the superlate-night clubs. The door to the incinerator room was only a few feet past the last storage locker, with the laundry room in the middle of the row; when she fed the flames, they always flared up, and experience had taught her the fire could draw inquisitive neighbors like hungry cockroaches—they seemed to come right out of the walls.

Not tonight, though. Elektra had the room all to herself, just her and the flames and all the things, large and small, that had made up her life. If possessions were worth anything as disposal objects, she'd burned so much she thought she ought to never have to take another job.

When the last bag had disappeared into the cleansing fire, Elektra checked again to make sure no one was around, then slipped out of the clothes she was wearing. The basement air was chilly against her bare skin but it felt good, very free. Her old clothes went into the fire with the previous bags, then she dressed in the brand-new travel clothes that McCabe had packed into the expensive Prada bag. Everything fit beautifully, but then she had expected no less. Also inside the bag was a wallet containing a set of newly forged ID cards and plenty of cash. These items she pocketed, then she held up the designer bag and inspected. The thing had probably cost six hundred dollars—what a shame. Elektra tossed it into the incinerator and thought McCabe would have been more frugal had he just gone to Wal-

Mart. Finally she pulled out her key ring and, after pulling a lone gold key from it, threw it in after the bag.

It took another fifteen minutes of monitoring the flames to be absolutely sure, and she did so without complaint or emotion crossing her face. Inside the conflagration was everything she was and had made herself out to be these past several months. She had stretched out this job, playing with DeMarco in three or four different locations, letting the murderous man think about the fact that she was coming for him and his days were numbered before he met his maker and answered for his crimes. Now DeMarco was dead and all traces of herself and her previous existence had to be obliterated, burned away to nothing but ashes and a quickly fading memory.

Once again, Elektra was nothing but a ghost.

5

HARBOR ISLAND, PACIFIC COAST

THE MORNING BREEZE WHIPPED AROUND ELEKTRA, dragging her hair up and making it seem to float around her head. The air was salty and laden with moisture, on the ragged edge of being cold. She stood at the railing of the ferry and waited while the other passengers loaded up, biding her time and searching for that spot inside herself that had once learned patience. Growing up . . . and dying . . . in New York had a way of stripping that out of a person, and she'd been surprised and secretly pleased when she'd read the location of her next job. It might be the off-season and cold on Harbor Island, but Elektra was looking forward to it. Fewer people, no traffic at all, and the sea, surrounding the small barrier island—with her on it—like a mother enfolding a wayward child and bringing her back to safety. There was, of course, a job to do . . . but she would think about that later. Right now, she could just enjoy the sea and the smell and the briny air saturating her body and her soul.

The island itself wasn't much, a mini-slice of paradise situated on what had once been nothing more than a sand bar off the Pacific coast. Now it was a remote vacation destination with no cars and no strip malls—just sand, surf, and beach homes that ran from the original hundred-grand weatherbeaten almost-shacks to multimillion-dollar summer mansions. There were only a handful of passengers besides herself, testament to what most tourists would consider damned lousy winter weather. That meant she was standing here with mostly year-rounders, fishermen and the occasional groundskeeper come to check on an employer's property, the truly random tourist family determined to bargain hunt, and the rare shopkeeper who kept his tiny business open throughout the year and refused to live elsewhere even when he had no more than one or two customers a day. Elektra loved it.

Fishing boats lolled in the harbor as the ferry's horn bellowed and the boat finally pushed off. Standing at the bow with her hair and a brightly colored scarf streaming behind her, Elektra could almost fantasize that she wasn't Elektra at all, but one of those ancient wooden female figureheads, the kind that was fastened to the front of the old sailing ships and led the crew's way through the most dangerous of seas.

Almost.

One of the boats angled into her view, blowing away her fantasy and pulling Elektra back to the here and now. It was a small rig, and on deck was a lone fisherman, a good-looking guy wearing all-weather gear who looked perfectly at home on his boat. Without meaning to, Elektra's eyes met his, and for a moment she found herself trapped by his dark gaze; in another instant, she turned away. She wasn't interested in flirting with anyone, and certainly not in an actual relationship. Ghosts didn't get involved with other people, and they didn't fall in love. They stayed away and uninvolved. They stayed *free*.

It was another two hours by the time the ferry made its run to the island proper, its passengers disembarked, and Elektra was done with the traveling part of her trip to Harbor Island. Calling a cab on a tiny offshore island wasn't nearly as easy as it was on the mainland, so that added more time until she could get to the beach house, kick off her shoes and unpack her few new belongings. She'd barely gotten the last new shirt put away when her cell phone rang, and she couldn't help looking at it in irritation before she went on and answered the thing.

"Yeah."

"How's the view?"

Elektra's lip turned up slightly in annoyance. Was she that predictable that McCabe would know she would already be walking out onto the deck with the phone in her hand? She paced along the deck's length like a tiger in a cage with unseen bars, ignoring the sight of the water and its crashing waves and watching her reflection in the walkway's mirrored panels. The same measured number of steps in one direction, the same in the other, then back again. She didn't even realize what she was doing.

"Lovely," she said shortly. Some distant part of her brain grumbled at this, wanting to share the truth—the house, with its gray-blue modern architecture and natural, wood-trimmed windows, was lovely. Pine trees framed it and thick potted plants lined the lower deck, while a glassed-in walkway let her see everything from the upper level. "You have details?"

"*Relax*," McCabe said. From twenty-eight hundred miles away, his voice was so clear he could have been inside the beach house with her. She could almost see his careless shrug as he said the next words. "*You wanted time off,*" he continued. "*Take some time.*"

Elektra shook her head even though he couldn't see her. No—the waiting was worse. She couldn't relax when there was something hanging over her head, a job waiting to be completed. "I just want to get this over with."

"*So you can do what?*" McCabe demanded. She opened her mouth to reply, but couldn't. She had no idea. There was that taking a vacation thing she'd contemplated before, but would she really? Ever? "*I'll call when I get the name.*" The cell phone clicked as McCabe broke the connection, but not before Elektra caught the undisguised annoyance in his voice. She closed the phone and went back inside, then decided it was time to familiarize herself with her new living space. She didn't know how long she'd be here—maybe a day, a week, maybe two or three months (which would drive her absolutely insane)—so it might as well be livable . . . which was not necessarily the same as comfortable. It was kind of eerie the way the inside of this place mirrored her last one, and the one before that, and the one before *that*. Not the exact layout, of course, but close. The furniture was similar, too—simple and elegant lines, easy-care—as were the colors from top to bottom, the few low-maintenance but home design plants scattered here and there.

It didn't take long to figure out where everything was and unpack the half dozen boxes of newly purchased household items that McCabe had sent. Flatware and dishes in the kitchen, a few cooking utensils she would rarely use; sheets and towels she found in a small linen closet outside the master bedroom, so she made up the bed, vaguely registering the freshly laundered scent as she smoothed out the last of the folds in the sheets. She tucked her old leather case into the master bedroom closet next to a tall box that was already there, then turned in the middle of the bedroom to give it a final inspection. All finished, everything in order.

When she stopped her visual examination, she found herself looking out the window at the ocean. It was nearing noon now, and the sun was glinting off the water's surface and making it look like simmering, liquid gold. Yeah, Elektra thought. A swim would be just the thing to take her mind off the upcoming job and kill a little time.

One of the things she'd unpacked earlier was a bikini, and she dug it out now and looked at it critically before changing into it. Red, of course, a sleek little thing made of faux red leather with a laced seam between the breasts that she had found amusing because it so closely resembled her assassin's costume. She didn't bother bringing a robe, towel, or shoes as she headed to the water—all those things would just be excess baggage, items she'd have to keep track of and worry that the wind, which was quite brisk out here, would fling away.

Not far from the back of the house was a pier leading out into the water, and it was this she chose to use so she could dive into the frigid water rather than walk in from the shore and have to endure the coldness creeping up her ankles. That was way too much like death; as with a lot of things, she'd rather just get it over with.

Elektra took the last ten feet of the pier at a dead run, then leapt off the end of it, pushing her body up and into an arc before curving down and neatly splitting into the waves. It was cold but she didn't care; down here was like another world, dark green and filled with echoing, distorted sounds. Then, for some reason, the light around her changed suddenly as she started to surface, brightening to something much more familiar, much more blue—

She broke the surface and blinked away the sunlight, splashing in surprise at the chlorine-scented water of the indoor swimming pool. Frightened, she dragged air into her lungs and dove under again, searching for the deeper green of the Pacific Ocean, the natural saltwater scent and the sting of the cold—

A memory, Elektra thought almost wildly. That's *all*. She rotated her body and stared upward, seeing the sun sparkling through the blue-green water overhead. Feeling better, she spread her arms and felt the ocean water's resistance against the surface of her skin as she propelled herself along horizontally, staying underwater until her lungs demanded oxygen. More confident now, Elektra scissored her legs and angled upward, pushing up and into the cold air—

She was eight years old, and already training in the martial arts. Strong for her size, determined and stubborn, but even she sometimes ran out of energy, even she sometimes just couldn't take anymore. The pool water was cool around her, but she was hot inside, overheated by the effort of treading water for so long with her thumbs held above the water's surface, keeping herself upright by the power of her child's legs alone. Her father, Nicholas, stood at the edge of the pool and watched her with an eagle's eye, making sure she didn't slip, that she didn't rest. Her mother, leaning back in a lounge chair, watched from a few feet away.

"Keep pedaling," her father ordered. "Five more minutes."

But she was so tired, so small. She wanted so much to please him, but even so, she could feel her hands sinking, over and over. Each time she would bring them back up and try to keep them there, but they never stayed that way; each time they fell back below the surface of the pool.

"No!" her father yelled at her. "No hands, Elektra! Don't be lazy—only use your feet!"

She pushed upward again, felt her hands drop.

"Don't be a girlie! Come on—let's go!" He was ranting now, driving her on and on and on. "Push, push, PUSH!"

She could feel her body giving out, her leg muscles burning until the limbs were too heavy to move. Even so, even as she sank and swallowed water, then came back up, sputtered and sank again, those same exhausted eight-year-old's legs tried to do what her father wanted, trying to propel her upward again and again and again. . . .

She surfaced again and thankfully found herself out of the old memory. To drive the last of it away, Elektra swam hard for the shore, pushing herself to her limit, cutting through the water like a shark. The outside air tingled against her already cold skin but it felt invigorating rather than freezing, one more thing she could use to ground herself in the here and now and leave the past behind. She shook the water out of her hair as she climbed the stairs to the beach house, sending salt-laden droplets in every direction. She was reaching for the doorknob when she froze.

Someone was inside.

Elektra's acute hearing easily picked up the footsteps and listened as someone lightweight moved quickly down the length of the living room. Without making a sound, her hand twisted the knob and pulled open the door only enough for her to slip inside the house, then she shut it silently behind her. The living room was draped in muted shadows, lit only by the heavily filtered light striping through blinds closed to keep out the intense midday sun. A quick glance to the right and Elektra picked out a box cutter lying next to a wad of tape she had yet to throw out. She moved toward it on the balls of her feet, shifting her weight and feeling the floor like a predatory cat stalking the bird that would soon become its next meal. In another two seconds Elektra had the box cutter in hand, up and aimed, and before the figure even knew there was someone else in the room, she whipped it through the air.

Thunk!

Elektra heard a gasp of surprise right before she reached over and snapped on the lamp on one of the end tables.

"Jesus!"

Elektra folded her arms and regarded the girl who

was staring at where the sleeve of her jacket was firmly pinned against the wall by the blade of the box cutter. She was in her early teens, maybe thirteen or fourteen, with a roundish face and shoulder-length dark blonde hair. The teenager scowled and tried to pull her arm free, but the weapon didn't budge. "What's the matter with you?" she demanded. "You could've killed me!"

Elektra ignored the complaint and glared at her uninvited visitor. "What are you doing here?"

"Nothing," the girl said petulantly. Then, as if she knew that wasn't going to fly, she added, "I'm friends with the Wheelwrights." She looked at her sleeve again, then reached over with her other hand and yanked out the box cutter. "Damn—you cut my friggin' jacket!"

She tossed her head and turned like she was going to walk out in a huff, but she hadn't completed her first step before Elektra's hand shot out and wrapped around her wrist. "How did you get in?" Elektra asked. She was careful to keep her voice calm, to hide—for now—the fact that she was absolutely furious.

The girl whirled with the box cutter raised and ready to strike, but again, she never got the chance. Elektra's other hand was nothing but a blur in front of the teen's face; there was a deceptively small *slap!* against the thumb pad of her hand, then her fingers went numb and released the weapon of their own accord. Elektra caught it reflexively and tossed it out of reach. The teenager gaped at her, then swallowed. "Th-the door w-was unlocked," she stammered. Her eyes were wide. "So I . . ."

"No, it wasn't," Elektra interrupted. Her voice was as frigid as the water dripping out of her hair.

They stared at each other, but Elektra wasn't giving in. "It *was*," the girl insisted. "The beach door."

Still maintaining a death grip on the slender wrist, Elektra began steering the teen toward the door on the beachfront deck off the master bedroom.

"The people who live here, they let me come all the time," the girl told her. Her voice was jittering. "Ask anybody."

Elektra paid no attention—she wasn't hearing anything useful anyway. The lock on the beach door *was* broken, but by whom? And when? The answer could easily be standing right in front of her, or it could have been that way all along. The girl chattered nervously on, but Elektra wasn't listening as her gaze roamed the room. She took in everything, subconsciously counting as she scanned the doors, the windows, the furniture. Something was odd, missing.

"So who are you?" the teenager asked. "My name is—"

Elektra yanked her forward. "What did you steal?"

Her visitor's face twisted. "Nothing! What do you think I am—*ow!*"

The hand she had kept rolled into a fist flew open as

72

suddenly Elektra squeezed it hard, digging the tip of her middle finger deep into the groove between the wrist bone and the median nerve. A necklace fell to the floor and bounced against the carpet, a necklace that was *very* precious to Elektra.

The girl couldn't meet her gaze. "Don't call the cops," she implored. "Please? My Dad'll *kill* me."

Elektra's scowl softened as she realized this girl had a family somewhere, a father and mother, maybe siblings. She'd probably just wandered in and seized the opportunity to explore a little, then found temptation stronger than common sense. She let go of the girl's wrist and bent to pick up her necklace. "In some parts of the world," Elektra told her, "they'd just cut your hands off and—"

The teenager shot for the door.

Foolish girl that she was, she was pretty surprised when Elektra was already waiting for her when she got there.

The quasi-thief's mouth dropped open. "*Whoa!* How did you—" She looked at Elektra speculatively. "Work out much?"

"Just get out of here," Elektra snapped, instantly angry at herself for revealing too much. "*Go.*"

This time the girl's common sense *did* win, and Elektra didn't have to repeat herself. She watched her go and squeezed the necklace, then thought about something else. Dropping the necklace back on the dresser, she hurried to the master bedroom closet and pulled open the door, but the leather case and box inside were untouched. Relieved, she let the door close once more, then wandered back over and stared at the ankh necklace the girl had tried to steal.

Today, it seemed, was a day for memories.

6

THE NATCHIOS ESTATE, A LONG TIME AGO

SHE'S BEEN IN THE POOL AGAIN, SEVERAL TIMES THAT day. At least this time was better than the last, her attempt at treading water much stronger and more successful, worthy of even her father's hard-won praise. Elektra is almost prancing, she feels so good, so rather than go through the changing room that connects to the kitchen, she heads for the main entrance. A quick skip across the fancy, complex pattern of tiles around the pool deck, then she crosses the lush, meticulously manicured lawn that separates the pool area from the front of the huge mansion that she and her family call home. She will make a grand, proud entrance, and she can't wait to tell her mother how well she's done at her exercises today. She'll—

The front door to the house is wide open.

Puzzled, Elektra stands in the foyer and looks around, but no one's there—not her parents, nor any of the servants, or even a visitor. After a few indecisive moments, she climbs the long, curving staircase that leads to the second floor. The polished oak steps are well made and don't make a sound beneath her slight weight; at the top of the staircase, she turns left and heads for the master bedroom suite. With her eyes focused on the door, Elektra nearly steps in the thick pool of blood that is seeping from beneath.

She skids to a stop and stares at the crimson puddle creeping into the fabric of the carpet, feeling terror rush into her throat and build a lump that threatens to cut off her breathing. There is so much of it, and it's so dark—surely it must be paint, some new creative project that her mom was trying and which had gotten the best of her. People didn't have that much liquid inside them.

Did they?

Her heart is thundering in her chest, the sound of her own blood rushing so loudly through her arteries that she can barely hear her own small voice as she timidly pushes open the bedroom door.

"M-mom?"

Something big and black—a demon!—hisses and shrieks at her. Elektra screams and throws herself backward, instinctively levering herself out of the swipe the thing takes at her face. Before she can react or run, the demon launches itself onto the windowsill where the curtains are billowing in the fresh summertime air. It turns and growls something at her, then jumps, and it isn't until she puts both hands behind her to push off that Elektra realizes she had ended up kneeling in the blood. She gasps and gets up anyway, wiping her hands automatically on her legs and succeeding only in

76

spreading it farther. She stumbles forward, looking around wildly, until she gets to the edge of the king-size bed—

And sees her mother lying there.

She's dead, her body the source of the blood that had gathered and crawled across the carpet to the doorway. Her head is thrown back above the wide path of red that leaks from beneath her corpse, and in her beautiful face her eyes—the same color as Elektra's—are open but she isn't seeing her daughter, or anything else, anymore.

Elektra's throat hitches and she feels tears sting behind her eyelids, but she will not allow herself to cry. Quietly, as though her mother were only sleeping, Elektra reaches over and lifts her mother's necklace from her throat. It's a small ankh, a symbol that her mother was never without; Elektra will keep it forever and ever. . . .

Amen.

PRESENT DAY, HARBOR ISLAND

At two a.m. Elektra woke up shaking and sweating and remembering, and hating the memories and herself for bringing the badness back to rattle around in her head. Her eyes were wide open and her mind was crawling around old stuff, bad stuff, jobs completed and people left dead for both good and bad reasons. Funny how tired she could be, limbs leaden and slow and blood so thick and sluggish that it felt like her heart couldn't even pump the stuff, but still she was wide awake, her gaze skimming the darkness like a female mosquito hunting for fresh blood in the middle of the night.

She made herself get up and go in the bathroom, found the new bottle of sleeping pills McCabe had made sure was packed with her move-in items. With only the night-light on, she swallowed two of the tablets without bothering to get a glass of water, staring at her faint reflection in the mirror as her throat worked the pills downward. Finally she went back in the bedroom and climbed into bed.

The pills didn't help—if anything, they just made her mind more slave than controller of her imagination. By two-thirty she could have sworn she was looking at DeMarco only a few feet away, still sitting on the chair in which he'd died across from his fancy fireplace . . . except now it was in Elektra's beach house bedroom. She could see her *sai* still jammed into his chest, conveniently preventing him from squeezing the trigger of that dangerous little Heckler & Koch with which he'd planned to kill her. She stared at him for a while, knowing that the whole thing had to be some sort of sleep-deprivation hallucination, but it didn't go away. Fine—if DeMarco wouldn't leave, she would. She rolled out of bed and walked out of the bedroom, purposely staring at the carpet instead of the dead man who couldn't possibly be there.

By three-fifteen she was pacing the floor again, back

and forth, this time in the living room. A sudden shriek made her whirl—it sounded so much like the one in the memories she had of her mother's bedroom on the day of her death. But no . . . it was just the teakettle, sounding the alarm that the water was boiling. Nerves jangling, Elektra made herself a steaming cup of vanilla-tinged chamomile—the stuff was supposed to relax you and lull you to sleep—then shed her sleep clothes in favor of comfortable workout garb. It didn't take long to fire up some music on her portable CD player, good hard stuff with a nonstop, driving beat that kept pace with her as she did a high-speed jump rope routine. If evil was sweat, then the tea and the workout raised her body temperature and helped to drive away the personal demons, at least for a little while. It wasn't long before her skin was glistening and her clothes were soaked.

By four a.m. she was working on her arms and upper body, counting out her numbers with excruciating slowness, gasping and trembling with the effort of hauling her body weight upward using only one arm—

"Forty-eight . . . forty-nine . . . *fifty*."

Elektra let go of the overhead bar and allowed herself to drop to the carpet. For a long while she simply stood there, waiting for the burn in her muscles to subside and for her heart rate to come down a bit, stop its jackhammering inside her chest so she could get on with the next part.

Finally she felt strong enough again.

She looked up at the bar, then leaped and gripped it with the other hand.

"One . . . two . . . three . . ."

Still in her workout clothes, Elektra was lying diagonally across the bed when the sun crested the horizon and the first of its rays bounced off the water. Despite the sleeping pills, the tiredness, the brutally difficult workout, there had been no sleep for her last night, just as happened more often than not. Once again, rest had eluded her, and she certainly wouldn't find it with the sunshine burning its way through her windows and her eyelids. Exhausted and sore, she dragged herself up and off the bed; as she pushed through the beach door and into the moisture-laden morning air outside, she felt like some strange cross between Sisyphus and a zombie.

She wasn't sure how long it took her to get there, but eventually Elektra found herself walking along a section of the beach that was awash in driftwood. It must have been something about the current and the tide that did it, but twisted pieces of the stuff lay everywhere, like the inexplicable skeletons of alien creatures for which humans had no name. She lost herself for a while as she walked among the wood carcasses, examining the ruins and quietly searching. Finally she found it—a nice, wide tree stump, one large enough for her to settle comfortably on in a cross-legged position. A moment later Elektra closed her eyes, and relaxed for the first time since she stepped off the ferry onto Harbor Island.

Her breathing slowed, and her muscles, so twisted inside that they might have been unintentional mock-ups of the knurled wood around her, finally untensed. Her spine was straight, her shoulders were pulled back, and her face was up to catch the air, pull it in and in and into her lungs, cleansing and cold. With each passing moment her inhalations were fewer, her heart rate slowed a little more, until finally everything met and meshed, becoming one as the sun warmed her shoulders and the breeze lifted her long hair.

Finally, she had it—kimagure. A sixth sense accessible only with the deepest of concentration, it enabled her to accurately perceive the world around her without even opening her eyes. She could feel the breeze, smell the salt water, hear the birds . . . and see well beyond the small stump on which she sat even though her eyelids were completely closed. Everything around her was moving, alive, even though to the untrained human eye it was nothing but a simple beach landscape dotted with dried-up tree limbs. She could sense the clouds in the sky, darkening as they approached and the weather changed. In her thoughts, the rain began to fall but her skin remained dry—what she was seeing was the rain that hadn't yet arrived.

Once, standing on a rooftop and facing Matt Murdock—Daredevil—he had told her the same thing: The rain was coming. She hadn't believed him, but his senses, attuned to the world differently than hers because of his blindness, had been completely correct. She learned later that he had used that sense to "see" her in his own way, forming images based on the echoing of the raindrops like a bat's sonar.

Like Matt, Elektra could see it all now, the totality of everything around her, even the future.

Which showed a man walking down the beach toward her.

She knew that he had seen her already, sitting on the stump like some kind of cold sun goddess, or maybe a female incarnation of Buddha. Even so, the instant he turned his head to glance at the waterfront, she was up and off the stump, and by the time he reached where she'd been sitting, he had no idea where she'd gone. She let him stand there and look puzzled for an amusing ten seconds, then stepped up behind him.

"Looking for me?"

"Oh!" He spun, surprise flashing across his features. Elektra recognized him instantly—the fisherman she'd seen smiling up at her from the smaller lobster boat. "Hi," he managed, then added, "Are you, uh, the new tenant?" When she frowned, he said, "Eddie Ferris— he's the Realtor—he said a young woman had taken the house, the one you're in, for a month."

Elektra didn't return his smile. "What do you want?"

She was being rude, but that was intentional. She watched as he tried a smile, but it wavered a little when her expression still didn't change. He glanced around, his eyes searching the beach. "Sorry," he said. He hesitated, then looked toward the beach again. "This is kind of awkward, but . . . have you seen a girl? She's thirteen, blondish-brownish hair down to about here?" He gestured at his shoulders self-consciously. At Elektra's curious expression, he explained, "My daughter, Abby. We had a fight yesterday morning. She took off, and I—"

"I saw her late in the afternoon," Elektra said.

The fisherman's eyes brightened. "You did? Thank God—"

Elektra decided to be blunt. "Yes. She broke into my house."

"Shit," he said crudely, then blushed a little. "Really? She knows the Wheelwrights, who own—say, she didn't take anything, did she?"

Elektra hesitated, then said "No." This one time, and *only* this one time, she decided, she would give the girl a break. If she did it again, though, Elektra would hang her out to dry.

He looked relieved. "Oh, good." He stared at the ground uncomfortably. "Look, if she broke anything, I'm happy to pay for it, of course. I'm Mark Miller. We're in the little cabin two properties down."

Elektra only folded her arms, not bothering to introduce herself. Mark smiled tightly and began to back away—obviously he wasn't an idiot and he was getting her hint. "Okay, well, thanks again. If you see Abby, could you ask her to at least call? I mean, she's probably around here and just avoiding me. She's good at that sometimes. I just need to hear from her."

Elektra barely nodded. His face grim, Mark turned and headed back the way he'd come, and she couldn't help but feel sorry for him.

7

ELEKTRA MADE HERSELF RELAX WHEN SHE REALized she was gripping her cell phone so tightly that her fingers were actually hurting. "Come on," she muttered. "Come on, come on, come on." Finally there was a click as the phone was picked up. She opened her mouth, then a slightly tinny version of McCabe's voice cut her off. "I'm out. Leave a message."

She didn't leave messages, so she snapped her phone closed and looked around for something else to do. She hoped to God she got the name of her target pretty soon, or she was going to go out of her mind with boredom.

She killed a couple of hours with some magazines that McCabe had thoughtfully packed into her new belongings, but they were more annoying than entertaining, filled with inanely material things that she would never possess. It wasn't the physical stuff, like furniture, clothes, or even a house with a stupid white picket fence—she had enough money socked away in foreign accounts to practically start her own town. It was the intangible things, like love, the joy of another's company, and the supposedly emotional peace it provided . . . which, of course, led to marriage, children, happily ever after, golden anniversaries, and yadda yadda yadda. Had there ever been a time when such things had been her goal, or any kind of a priority at all in her life? She'd known love with Matt, but that had been too brief and had ended in false betrayal, mistaken accusations, and her nearly killing him . . . right before her own death. She couldn't imagine going through something like that again, and she certainly wasn't the kind of woman who could slide into an everyday suburban life.

At dusk, Elektra tossed the magazines aside and headed outside to the deck, the part that overlooked the big boulders just beyond the house where the sun would set. Facing west, she stood and enjoyed the wind and the way it carried the salt spray from the waves over her face. It was cold enough to be biting but she didn't care; the froth of the breaking waves was stark white against the dark water, and the clumps of clouds were painted brilliant pink and red by the sun's final rays. You didn't get spectacular sunsets like this in New York, where—

"Hey."

Elektra spun in surprise, then saw Abby standing over by the door. Chagrined, she scuffed her way across the deck toward the girl. "How long have you been standing there?"

Abby shrugged. "Like a minute."

Elektra managed to hide her frown, but that bothered her—usually *she* was the one who crept up on people, not the other way around. How had this child managed to do just that?

Abby looked at her out of the corner of her eye. "What'd you tell my father? Did you tell him I broke into your house?"

"Yes." Elektra studied her. "Because you *did* break in."

Abby tossed her head. "You didn't have to *tell* him. I thought you were cool."

Elektra only looked at her. "I'm not."

Abby's lips pressed together. "No kidding. Now he's on my case. He made me come ask you to have Christmas dinner with us."

Elektra blinked. "Have what?"

Abby glanced at her in amazement. "Hello? Christmas dinner? As in December twenty-fifth?" When Elektra only looked blank, Abby rolled her eyes. "Come on, you do know what Christmas is, right?"

Elektra felt her cheeks redden. "Yes, of course I know."

Abby's laugh made Elektra realize the girl had been kidding, but there was still her next question to deal with, and she was completely serious. "Did you know *today* was Christmas?"

Elektra shrugged, but it was pretty clear that she

hadn't had a clue. In any event, there was something interesting about this teenager and Elektra was picking up on it—like now, Abby's gaze kept roaming over the outside of the beach house, sweeping back and forth, then doing it again.

"He's making crab," Abby continued. She didn't seem to know she was doing anything odd. "I *hate* crab. If you come, he won't notice me not eating it."

"Thank you, but I can't," Elektra said automatically. When the girl focused on her quizzically, Elektra felt like a fly caught in a spiderweb. "I . . . have something to do."

"What?" Abby asked immediately. Funny how teens had no qualms about asking the most personal questions. "Everything's closed. You're on an island." She flicked one hand toward the beach house, then the empty shore. "What do you have to do—work out some more?"

Elektra scowled and took a step toward Abby. "What, were you spying on me?"

Abby's eyes widened. "No!" She spread her hands. "Look at you—it's obvious you do that all the time. Come on, *please?* It's driving me crazy out here, every night, just the two of us . . ." She let her voice trail off and her gaze traveled over the house. "I'm bored."

Elektra tilted her head. "What are you doing?"

"Nothing." The teen jerked, as though she'd been

caught doing something she shouldn't. She met Elektra's gaze and frowned. "What?"

"Are you counting?"

Abby looked taken aback. "No."

A corner of Elektra's mouth turned up as she looked back at the house, noting the windows that overlooked the beach, the broad door, other, finer details. She turned once more to Abby, but the girl was back on the subject of Christmas dinner. "So will you come? *Please?*"

Now Abby's voice was downright plaintive, and Elektra found herself giving in. She inhaled deeply, but when her voice came out, instead of saying no, she said, "I have to change my clothes."

The teenager's smiled stretched across her face, brightening everything about her. "Thanks!" When Elektra nodded, she said, "I'm Abby."

Of course—Abby would have no idea that her father had already told Elektra her name. She swallowed, knowing Abby expected her to introduce herself, too. She didn't want to—the fewer the people who knew who she was, the better—but she couldn't figure out how *not* to. If she gave something false, she'd be discovered the first time Abby or Mark called to her and she didn't respond. Well, she was an assassin, not a spy, and there *was* a difference. "Elektra," she said reluctantly.

Abby smiled all over again, obviously approving.

"Elektra—cool." When Elektra moved toward the door, Abby seem to know ahead of time what was best. "I'll just wait out here," she said, and pointed to one of the lounge chairs. "Just don't take forever or I'll turn into an icicle."

Elektra nodded and resigned herself to having a holiday meal tonight, just like normal people.

When Abby pushed open the door to the cabin she shared with her dad, Elektra could see Mark over the girl's shoulder. He was working at the stove and doing an admirable job of it, too; with an oversized crab pot boiling on the back burner, he had the front burner going beneath a large skillet in which he was sautéing broccoli like a pro. The noise of the door opening made him look up, and his surprised expression was nearly comical. "Hey!" he snapped. "I told you *not* to leave the house!"

Abby sent her father a semi-withering look. "You didn't even know I was gone."

"Abby," Mark said in a warning voice. "I—"

"Chill, Dad," Abby said quickly. "We have a guest." She grabbed Elektra's arm and pulled her inside, then quickly reached behind her and pushed the door closed before Elektra could turn around and back out.

Talk about awkward—Elektra could've cheerfully throttled the girl. From the silence in the kitchen, it was obvious Abby had lied about the invitation coming from Mark, and now here was Elektra, the surprise holiday guest. She felt like somebody's mother-in-law dropping by on Saturday night without an invitation. "I'm sorry," Elektra said. "She said you were inviting me. I'll—I'll just—"

But Mark had already recovered from his shock. "No—no, please stay." The smile he sent her way was genuine, but she still hesitated. Boy, this was embarrassing. "I'm glad you're here," he added.

Okay, now she was stuck—she'd look like the female version of Scrooge if she turned up her nose at his invitation. Even so, this place was like a Norman Rockwell holiday painting—Christmas tree in the corner, a roaring fire. . . . Mark was even wearing a ridiculous reindeer cooking apron and matching oven mitts. God, Elektra couldn't have felt more out of place.

"So," Mark said cheerfully. "Can I get you a beer? Wine?"

Elektra swallowed. "Water," she answered. "Water would be great."

Abby pulled out one of the kitchen chairs, spun it, and sat on it like a boy. "Her's name's Elektra, Dad."

Mark nodded as he dug into the freezer and came out with a tray of ice cubes. "Elektra," he repeated. "Like the tragedy? Your parents must have had a sense of humor."

A sense of humor? She'd never had anyone suggest that before. "Not really."

Mark held out the glass of water and Abby took it before Elektra could accept it. The teenager gestured for her to follow her and her dad into the living room. Elektra obliged, watching as they glanced at each other. Something strange—a look, an unspoken message?—passed between those two, but Elektra had no idea what. This room continued the all-American family theme; besides the Christmas tree and fireplace Elektra had glimpsed when she'd arrived, the room was heavy with quilts and an early American theme. Elektra thought it was pretty obvious Mark decorated for Abby—or at least the way he *thought* he should decorate for her—rather than for himself. As she settled on the overstuffed couch with Abby, Mark headed back to the kitchen and promised dinner in another ten minutes. While she listened to Abby chatter on about the ornaments on the tree and where they'd picked up certain ones, the California coast, and a dozen other teenager-type things, Elektra thought this was going to be the longest ten minutes of her life.

It was a nice little spread and, as it turned out, Mark had cooked more than enough to allow for the addition of a last-minute guest. Elektra's generously loaded plate included freshly caught crabs boiled and served with melted butter, sautéed broccoli, and crusty French bread with more butter—no dieting on Christmas night, thank you. Off to the side was a mouth-watering salad which included a few of Elektra's traditional Greek favorites: feta cheese, Kalamata olives, lots of oregano, and even a few well-placed anchovy filets (which Abby turned up her nose at and carefully pushed aside).

Elektra found herself hungrier than she'd thought, and she wasn't sure if her appetite was up because of the company, the food, or both. She couldn't recall the last time she'd eaten a meal this large. Boredom had been chewing a good hole in her attitude and this was a welcome break, even if it had started off on a rocky foot. She was enjoying her food, and Abby's teenager-based chatter was strangely soothing . . . and more than a little revealing about the girl's tenacity.

" . . . so when she like sees that all the cute guys like *me*—just as friends, Dad—she *accidentally* spills poster paint all over my model of the Taj Mahal. So I put glue in her shoes, and then *I* got suspended for that. Then I got expelled for fighting, but that was back in the day in . . . uh . . . Baltimore."

When she hesitated, Abby glanced at Mark with a sort of *uh-oh* expression; that made Mark shoot a furtive glance at Elektra, who wisely pretended not to notice anything. Clearly trying to cover up for his daughter, Mark said quickly, "Quite a record, huh?"

Elektra smiled slightly, then looked at Abby. "Is there a school here on the island?"

Another hesitation, another glance at her father,

who again took over the conversation. "We're trying home schooling for a while."

"I read at college level," Abby said, as if she felt she needed to explain. "And I'm already doing algebra one on my own."

"She's a good student," Mark said. His tone of pride darkened a bit with his next sentence. "It's the behavioral stuff that's been a problem."

For a change, Abby looked sheepish. "I have . . . authority issues."

Mark laughed and shot Elektra a knowing glance. "She's heard this from the school psychologist," he said. He paused a moment, then looked at her expectantly. "So, I was a little surprised to see you take the Wheelwright place. Not many renters this time of year."

Elektra shifted uncomfortably on her chair. "I'm just here for the month. To work."

Abby's expression turned eager. "What do you do, anyway?"

Elektra tried to think quickly of a way to put what she did in terms that wouldn't make her an outright liar. That was bad karma, and there was always a way to phrase something delicately. "Like layoffs," she finally said. "Payroll reduction, that sort of thing."

Abby made a face. "Sounds boring."

"Abby . . ." Matt's tone was heavy with parental warning.

Elektra grinned purposely. "No, it *is* boring." Abby kept playing with something on her wrist and finally Elektra got a good look at it. Excellent—just want she needed: something to change the subject. "I like your bracelet, by the way. You know what those are?"

Abby stopped fingering it when she realized Elektra was watching her. "Uh . . ." She seemed a little self-conscious now that both her father's and Elektra's attention were fully focused on her.

"Warrior beads," Elektra told her. She nodded her head at the multiple strands wrapped around Abby's wrist. They glittered in the room's light as Abby held up her arm to show the carved silver and copper beads more clearly. A larger bead was in the center of the bottommost strand, very much like an end weight. They were rare, but Elektra had, occasionally, run across them. "They're from Indonesia. Centuries ago you had to be the best fighter in your village to earn them."

Abby looked from her to the bracelet on her slender wrist. "Huh," she said. "I bought it on eBay."

But her expression had gone from flustered to pleased, and Elektra wasn't sure if it was because of what was behind the bracelet, or because *Elektra* knew what the beads were.

Either was quite possible.

Later, Elektra would be surprised that the evening, which had started out slowly and painfully and about as promising as having her jaw wired shut, had passed so quickly. Mark and Abby's cabin was small, but it certainly had all the creature comforts, not only on the inside but outside as well. With her farewell to Abby already said, right now Elektra was standing on a small outside deck that faced the ocean; behind her was the window to Abby's room, through which she could see Mark tucking his daughter into bed and giving her a good-night hug.

Off to the side were a couple of well-padded deck chairs that looked a little too inviting—she should really be heading back to the beach house and her own space. But it was nice to surreptitiously watch Mark with his daughter, to see them like this. It gave her good, solid evidence that despite the bickering, the two were close and affectionate. He disappeared from view, and she turned to face the ocean, telling herself that she could spare five more minutes; this late at night, with what little there was of the moon obscured by the evening clouds, Elektra couldn't see the water. She could, however, hear the crashing of the surf, a sound both soothing and restless, never-ending.

Mark's footsteps came from behind her and made Elektra turn. He was standing there and smiling; in one hand he held a bottle of wine with a holiday label on it from a local winery, in the other, two festive-looking wineglasses. "Suddenly I have a teenager on my hands," he said apologetically.

Elektra nodded. "She's hard on herself."

Mark raised one eyebrow as he set the glasses on the deck railing, then pulled out a pocket corkscrew and went to work on the cork. "You can tell, huh?" He chuckled to himself but he looked pleased. "Most people think she's a slacker." In another second, he'd twisted the cork free and filled both glasses. He handed her one. "Here you go."

She reached for it automatically, but her hand wavered in midair after her fingers has closed around the stem. "No . . . I shouldn't."

He blatantly ignored her protest, instead touching his glass to hers in a toast. "Merry Christmas."

Another hesitation, but she could think of no good reason why she couldn't relax just a bit on this holiday night. Finally, she nodded at him and took a sip. Mulled spice, thick and rich, slightly sweet—probably a treasured recipe from the local vineyard, something only brought out once a year. Nice. "Where's her mother?" Elektra asked, hoping to keep the conversation from tumbling around back to her and sparking questions she couldn't—or wouldn't—answer.

Mark's face darkened. "She died about a year ago."

Elektra felt her throat tighten and she gave him a chance to continue. God, she knew firsthand how it felt to be Abby's age and lose your mother. "Back in Baltimore?" she asked when he didn't offer any more information.

"Yeah," he said hoarsely. "Drunk driver."

Elektra looked away for a long moment, then met his gaze again. "My mother died when I was young."

For a second, Mark looked almost comically surprised that she would share such a hugely personal piece of trivia about herself. "Really?" He looked at her, expecting more details.

But he wasn't the only one surprised—she should never have revealed so much. And now that she had, Elektra could tell he was gearing up to ask more questions, things she didn't want to go into. "I should go," she said abruptly. "I have a lot of work to do."

Mark's expression fell. "Oh, come on—it's early." He glanced back to the window on the other side of Abby's, where he could see the living room clock atop the fireplace mantel. She would never admit it aloud, but the inside *did* look inviting, filled with a warmth that had been too long missing from her life. But no, she couldn't let material things like that tempt her. Things like . . . normalcy. "It's only—"

"Thanks for dinner," Elektra said, cutting off his words. He glanced at his glass and when he looked up again, she was gone.

While she slipped into the shadows and headed down the beach and Mr. Mark Miller tried to figure out where she'd disappeared to, Elektra couldn't help puzzling over why his expression looked more worried than surprised about her leaving. . . .

8

THE COLD WIND ALONG THE SHORE FRONT HAD died away, leaving Christmas night—Elektra still couldn't believe she hadn't realized *that*—calm and silent. On one side the water was dark and still, waveless, and with the moon still concealed behind the clouds the ocean looked like a sheet of black ice stretching as far as the eye could see, shiny and ominous. On her other side, her sea-level perspective was enough to make the tiny island appear to stretch off into a blackness broken only by very occasional glints of night. There weren't many houses here, and most of those were dark and empty, their families gone to spend the winter in an area with more amenities and, given the affluence of the people who generally owned property here, probably a warmer climate. While Harbor Island could be pleasant enough during the day in December, she could easily picture people wintering in Florida, Mexico, or even Hawaii.

Holidays, it seemed, were invented not just for celebrations but to foster memories. As Elektra headed down the beach at her usual measured pace, she was helpless to prevent her mind from wandering back through the years, touching here and there on times both painful and happy—

Beyond the bridge entrance, the maze on her parents' estate was thick and green, and freshly cut—it smelled wonderful, like concentrated summer just released from a tightly stoppered bottle. She was supposed to be quiet or she'd be found out, but she couldn't, no matter how hard she tried, and when her mother's face peeked around a corner and their eyes met, young Elektra erupted into giggles and abandoned her attempts at stealth. Instead she ran full out, zipping around corners and laughing outright, her mother doing the same. It wasn't long before the elder Natchios caught up with her—well, she might have let her mother do that—and then Elektra waited, trembling and jittery with anticipation, as her mother gently tied a white blindfold across her eyes. With her hand tucked into her mother's elbow, Elektra let herself be led, and the sensation wasn't as disconcerting as she expected. She was walking blind and feeling her way, yes, but she knew this maze as well as the crew who had planted the hedges in it, knew every turn and corner and how many steps long each corridor was; when they stopped so her mother could untie the blindfold, Elektra already knew they were at the maze's center.

She was, however, surprised to find her father waiting for them . . . standing right next to a newly built wishing well.

"Oh, Daddy!" The circular well was beautiful, its waist-high walls hand-constructed of smooth river stones in a myriad of colors beneath a small roof of hardened cedar shingles. Elektra circled it, hopping up and down with excitement and happiness, then she threw herself into her father's arms and hugged him furiously. He held on to her in return, his arms strong and tight. With her mother looking on and smiling, Elektra had never felt so secure. Her father was still smiling when she pulled away, and she eagerly took the silver dollar piece he offered her—she had a big future to wish for, long and bright and happy, and she would need a big coin to cover it all. Concentrating so hard that she was just on the edge of frowning, Elektra finally tossed the big silver piece into the well, watching it arc upward before it fell, twinkling end over end, into the darkness at the well's center. . . .

A good memory, but by the time Elektra finally reached the beach house and climbed into bed, it was followed by one much darker and unwanted—

Elektra stood off to the side, watching silently as members of her father's staff worked together to drape dust covers over all the furniture in the house. Up and fluff, out and down. Up and fluff, out and down. They were quiet and efficient, talking in murmurs and being careful not to look in her direction. She followed them from room to room, starting with the foyer and working into each bedroom and the living room, counting each one without knowing it, watching as they spread the sheets in the air and let them flutter down like pallid, fragile snow ghosts that enveloped everything. They left only her father's study, glancing uneasily at each other as they passed the door without touching it, not noticing that Elektra, who had followed them everywhere until now, decided to stay behind.

When their footsteps had faded to nothing more than far-away thumps, Elektra grasped the handle of the study door and eased it downward, moving more quietly than she'd ever done in her life, more quietly than she'd ever thought she could. She felt the latch release beneath her hand but it made no sound, and she slipped into the room as if she were a ghost herself. This was a huge study, the room nearly as large as the library upstairs, and when she carefully pushed the door closed behind her, Elektra saw her father sitting at his desk nearly twenty feet away. His head rested on his hands and he looked almost as though he were sleeping, so she stayed in the shadows and just watched him. For a long time he didn't move, long enough so that she began to worry; when she crept closer, she realized his eyes were open and he was staring at something on his desk—two large swords with wicked-looking handles that ended in a sharp point on each side of the main hilt. What were they called? Sais, that's right. He had told her about them before.

He stood suddenly, and only a quick backstep into the shadows kept her from being seen. Where before his mood had seemed dark and introspective, now it looked like he had made up his mind about something. As Elektra watched, he picked up the two sais and strode over to the wall on the other side of the room, where the cherrywood cabinets were built in place from floor to ceiling. He took a key from his pocket and twisted it into the lock of one of the upper ones, then slid the two blades inside, pushing them at an angle so they'd fit. That done, he closed the cabinet door and locked it, then went back to his desk and tossed the key into one of the drawers. He gave the room a final look around, then reached out and turned out the lamp.

With the darkness now giving her even more camouflage, Elektra ducked out the door and scampered up the stairs before her father could notice she was in there.

Elektra opened her eyes in the bedroom and frowned at the darkness permeating the beach house, ears straining. No, there was nothing wrong—no sound, no visitors. Just her and a traitorous mind that kept bringing back old memories that she would so much rather leave buried . . .

Elektra's woolen funeral suit was black, heavy and uncomfortably itchy; the white blouse beneath it was starched to a fault, and every fold and crease dug into her sensitive skin and made her even more miserable than she already was. But she wouldn't be bothered by insignificant things like fabric today—there was something she had to do, a very important task she had to complete. It had taken her a few days to understand the why and wherefore of it, to realize that her father had decided not to avenge her mother's death, but she would have none of that. Maybe she couldn't do it now, but someday . . . oh, yes. And even though such a day was somewhere in a faraway and unseen future, Elektra already knew what she would need when she got there.

Her father was off somewhere, talking with some servant or another, planning the closure of the house, the ride to her mother's funeral, the wake where people would come to "pay their last respects." He didn't notice when she calmly walked out of the room, moving as though that was exactly what she was supposed to do. Last respects? This was something else young Elektra didn't understand—why did grown-ups wait to visit until the people they loved were dead? Why not visit and "pay their respects" while that person was still alive to receive them? To her, it made no sense, but there was little in her life these last few days that had.

The furniture in her father's study had been the last in the house to be draped, but his massive desk was still uncovered. Elektra hurried over to it and checked the drawers as quietly as she could, going through each one until she found the key she'd seen him put away the day before. Clutching it in her palm, she dragged one of the leather chairs over to the wall cabinets, then pulled the sheet aside and climbed on top of it. She had to stretch to get the key into the lock, and for a long three seconds she didn't think she'd be able to make it turn. Finally, though, there was a click and the cabinet door eased open.

The sais were heavy and dangerously sharp, and she took them out of the cabinet one at a time. Moving as quickly as she dared, Elektra relocked the cabinet and tossed the key back into the drawer, then moved the chair back to its place and positioned the sheet so that it looked like it had never been touched. Carrying both the sais was a struggle, but she would not give up—someday, she was going to need these.

It was bright outside, obnoxiously so. Today was her mother's funeral—shouldn't it be overcast? Pouring rain and thundering, crying from heaven? It always did that on television, but now that she was living the reality of it, Elektra realized it didn't matter. No matter how bright the sunshine, how warm the breeze and sweet the birdsong, she was so sad that all she wanted to do was curl up on the cool, green grass and cry.

But there was no time for that—she had to finish her task.

Elektra found her way to the center of the maze and the well without thinking about it, and for a moment after she'd dropped the sais on the ground, she just stood there and glared at it. Wishing well? Where was the future she'd wished for, all the happiness and stars, and the live-happily-ever-after? She was just a kid, but already she knew that all that had died with her mother.

Shaking her head, Elektra squatted and began digging into the soft ground next to the well, being extra careful not to dirty her suit or the white cuffs peeking out from beneath her jacket. When the hole was deep enough, she dragged the sais over and pushed them into it, making sure that no part of their bright metal showed through the soil she meticulously pressed into place over them.

"Elektra! Elektra, where are you?"

Her father—it must be time to leave for the funeral. She gave the ground a final, hasty smoothing over, then stood and brushed the dirt off her hands. If she had to, she could hide her dirty fingernails in her jacket pocket. She gave the well one last glance, then hurried to meet her father, wondering why, of all things, she could hear a telephone's muffled ringing in the maze—

Elektra sat up with a gasp and grabbed at the cell phone ringing on the nightstand. "What?" she demanded hoarsely.

"You just got a delivery," said McCabe.

She'd been dreaming, another nightmare; she was soaked with sweat and her feet were tangled in the sheets and she had to fight to get free. Cold, wet air blasted her in the face when she opened the door and looked down; between the outer storm door and the inside one was a manilla envelope—it was always amazing how McCabe could get something to her in the middle of the night, no matter where she was.

Back inside, she ripped open the envelope and dumped its contents on the table. For a long moment she was silent as she stared at what had been inside. Finally, because she knew McCabe was expecting some kind of comment, she said, "It's a double?"

"That's why the big bucks."

She didn't say anything back, just kept staring at the two photographs and the information sheets. They read like something out of a statistics class—cold and impersonal, height, weight, age, eye and hair color.

"*What's the matter?*" McCabe asked. She could hear the suspicion in his voice.

"Nothing."

"*Good,*" he replied, but she could tell he didn't believe her.

Functioning on autopilot, Elektra scanned the sheets of paper. "A kid?" she asked at last. "What'd the kid do?"

"*Talked back in class, had the wrong father, how would I know?*" McCabe's voice was getting more and more impatient. "*It's a job, E. When did you start asking questions?*"

"I'll call you when it's done," she said coldly, and hung up on him.

For a long time, Elektra simply sat there in the dark, head down and gaze fixated on the floor. Finally she made herself stand and go to the closet, where she pulled out the battered leather case. She carried it back to the living room and opened it, then almost reverently pulled out the fitted leather sheaths containing her sais. Working methodically, first she polished each blade with Simichrom, working it in with her fingers until the oil absorbed any dirt and turned dark. When that was wiped clean, she took a chamois and a tube of Japanese sword oil and meticulously oiled every exposed area until the two blades gleamed like new chrome in the low light of her living room.

That done, she sat back and waited for morning.

She was up and dressed in a red leather jacket and jeans before the sunrise, with her sais tucked comfortably into her sleeves. The morning sky was painted rose and gold by the coming sun, making everything look deceptively warm even though the air was still holding on to the previous night's chilly temperature.

Striding up the beach, almost marching, Elektra tried to keep her mind blank, tried to focus on the job at hand and block out all the doubts and guilt that wanted to inch their way into her brain. She didn't have time for things like that in her life, and certainly not in her line of work—assassins, *professional* ones, didn't feel doubts, guilt, or emotions. They got their job, they did what they were hired to do, they collected their money, and, if they were wise, then they disappeared. So far, she'd been very good at all of that.

Her pace picked up almost without her knowing it, but there was no outrunning the thoughts in her head. So be it—she would have to live with them, let them yammer away.

She could still do her job.

There was a small spillway behind the Miller cabin and Elektra used the sounds of the flowing water in it to disguise her approach. She ended up on a slight rise right by the kitchen window, which was more than adequate for her needs. She had a slanting view down and into the kitchen, and she could see both Mark and Abby as they moved around the house, passing in and out of her view as they got ready to meet the day. All she needed was a good shot—actually, *two* good shots—and then this job would be over and she could get on about the business of her life . . . whatever that was.

Elektra waited, a sai in each hand. It was only a few moments before Mark ambled across her view, then stopped in front of the window and turned his back, putzing around with something on the table, unknowingly lining himself up perfectly in her vision. It should have been the perfect shot, really, there was nothing at all wrong with it . . . but maybe she could wait for something better, something with the girl closer to the window so she could get them both with more speed.

In another blink of the eye, Abby stepped into view, standing next to her father, a classic case of actually *getting* what you wish for. Elektra's hands were frozen on her sais—she couldn't help listening to the warm, familiar banter between father and daughter, a casual conversation that showed affection and was never meant for someone outside the family to hear.

Mark moved, and Elektra heard the sound of a can clanking against something metal. He looked over and she saw him grin at Abby. "How about some canned plums?"

Even from this far away, Elektra could see Abby roll her eyes in amusement. "Dad, you are *such* a sugar junkie."

"What?" he asked defensively. "I used to love these when I was a kid."

Abby smiled but didn't say anything for a moment. Then, instead of talking about breakfast, she asked, "When am I gonna see Grandma?"

Elektra saw Mark's shoulders rise as he inhaled. "I don't know, honey. Soon . . . I hope. Soon."

Crouching above the window, Elektra pressed her lips together, growing more and more angry with herself for not just *doing* it, taking the two shots and getting this over with. But no, the timing wasn't right, something wasn't right . . . at least that's what she tried to convince herself of as she finally moved away from the window. Still telling herself she could go with the shots, aloud she was muttering to herself. "Come on, *damn* it—just . . . push. *Push*." She started to repeat herself, but all her air was gone, and she just

couldn't

do it.

Out of the corner of her eye as she left, she saw Mark and Abby suddenly freeze. Had they sensed her out there? Had they *heard* her?

Without warning, Abby spun, fast, and made for the door. Her dad grabbed her before she could get there.

"Dad, let me," she said urgently. "I'm—"

Time to go.

He shook his head. "Stay here," he told her as he leaned over the sink and peered out the window.

But by the time he focused on the foliage outside, there was nothing to see but empty green, and nothing for him to do but exchange worried glances with his daughter.

Enough of this, Elektra thought as she stormed back into the warm front room of the beach house. She was absolutely furious with herself for not being able to do what she was supposed to. For God's sake, it was almost as if she couldn't even *think* the phrase, use the words in her own mind. Well, damn it, she could—she had to *kill* them, both of them. She was the assassin—the *paid* assassin—and they were her targets. She'd never met them before yesterday, and she shouldn't care if they were alive tomorrow.

She strode to the closet and yanked out the tall box, then pried it open and began assembling the contents. The Martin Cougar Elite compound bow took shape rapidly beneath her experienced hands, and she barely had to think about what went where. This one had a hand-held trigger and a telescopic sight that made it almost as accurate as a firearm and could send an arrow off at nearly three hundred feet per second. She hated herself for admitting a weakness, but maybe if she could put some distance between her and her two marks—

enough to where she didn't have to hear them chatter at each other and therefore didn't have to remember that they were *people*, people with whom she'd shared a Christmas dinner—maybe then she could do her job and end it the way she ought to.

With a final tightening of the limb bolts, Elektra shouldered the Martin and stood. As she grabbed a half dozen aluminum arrows, Elektra realized she'd be leaving a mess, a telltale sign of her presence here, if she didn't clean up.

Too bad. She couldn't worry about that right now. Right now she had to do something to stop the erosion of her own abilities.

Right now, she had to kill.

It took her less than five minutes to get back to Mark's property, although this time she was well out of range of hearing, no matter how sensitive either of them might be. They were such innocent victims, the worst kind—only the inexperienced kept their curtains spread wide, only the most ignorant didn't realize that doors and windows should be locked and covered at all times. As they had earlier, Mark and Abby wandered at will across the line of Elektra's sight, easy prey for the killer neither had any idea was waiting outside.

Down on one knee, Elektra brought up the compound bow and pulled back on the bowstring, inhaling as she pulled against a nearly sixty-five pound draw weight. Mark was easy to fix in the center of the sight and Elektra's hand was steady as she watched him; his back was to her again and rather than release the arrow, Elektra found herself wondering what he was doing. Paying a bill, chopping up a snack for Abby to eat, or spooning out those canned plums he'd talked about earlier this morning?

Elektra frowned but kept the bowstring pulled taut against her cheek. One more second and—

Abby stepped into the center of the window—obviously their nervousness of this morning had dissipated. She said something to her dad and he looked over at her and smiled; at that, Abby stepped slightly behind him and put her arm casually across his shoulders.

Now would be good, no, now would be *perfect*. They were at a slight angle to her and she could get them both with one shot, accurate enough to pierce both their hearts and likely kill them instantly. Very little pain, no fuss—

Abby's arm dropped away and Mark stepped to the left, disappearing from Elektra's view. Abby stayed where she was, looking downward. Maybe she was reading something, a magazine article her dad had noticed and told her about, a letter, a strip of brightly colored comics, *any*thing. She was right there, centered in the kitchen window and in Elektra's telescopic sight, motionless and so very vulnerable. An easy target, over in a flash—

Elektra's arm began to tremble from the pull of the bowstring. Ten seconds later she still hadn't fired and the tremble turned into a full shake as her muscles hit their fatigue point.

Finally, Elektra eased the bowstring forward and lowered the bow.

"I'm not doing it."

There was a moment of stunned silence on the other end, very rare for McCabe. He was a man who always had something to say, usually a comment sarcastic enough to annoy the person on his receiving end. Elektra kept up her momentum and her routine, flipping rapidly through her key ring until she found the only one she wanted before tossing the others into one of several filled plastic garbage bags on the floor.

"You mean now? Or ever?"

She kept moving, although even to herself she thought it was a little overboard. After all, she'd only been here for two days, barely time enough to use any of this stuff. On the other hand, she *had* unpacked it, which meant she had handled every single item she'd removed from a box. Yeah, best to bleach it or throw it all out just like she always did. "Too many variables," she said into the cell phone. "Not enough background."

"What do you need background for?" McCabe asked irritably. *"You kill them, they're dead."* He sighed. *"How*

about born in Minnesota, July ninth, a Leo. Is that enough?"

He was being sarcastic and she didn't need to explain herself to him—hell, she *couldn't*. Rather than argue, she said, "I'm out of here. I'll call you when I land someplace."

As she was closing the telephone, her sharp hearing picked up McCabe's voice, and the last words in the world she needed to hear:

"They'll just send someone else."

Elektra put it out of her mind and started dragging the garbage bags across the floor so she could throw them away.

9

THERE WAS A STORM BREWING OVER THE OCEAN.

Elektra could feel it, not just in the air but in her own body. Despite the humidity and salt-laden air, the ends of her hair crackled, and the finer hair on her arms was raised, charged by the static electricity in the air. There were huge thunderheads over the water, towering over the tiny island like cotton monoliths, and the wind screaming across the ocean surface did nothing to push them away. They boiled overhead, black and gray colors battling it out for dominance.

She wasn't the only one waiting for the ferry. With the storm quickly approaching, even on post-Christmas night most of the island's off-season residents had opted to travel back to the mainland and more stable ground to wait it out.

Finally the ferry was there, inching its way up to the loading dock. There were a few cars on it, maybe islanders gone mainland for Christmas dinner with relatives and who were now returning, some of the ferry's crew. Waiting her turn to get on, Elektra wrapped her scarf tighter around her neck and scanned the people automatically. Her gaze skipped over the usual fisherman and the captain, then rested on two men wearing black sunglasses despite the day's storm-induced dimness. Elektra frowned and glanced right and left—just checking—but when she looked back, the two oddballs were gone.

No, something wasn't right. She could forgive the glasses—lots of people had supersensitive eyes or just didn't like daylight, whether it was cloudy or not. But Elektra's nerves were singing now, sending unpleasant little pulses of warning signals across her shoulders and to her brain. She had to find out.

Another quick glance around, then Elektra closed her eyes and concentrated, dropping into kimagure at a speed only successful because of purest necessity.

Abby was screaming.

The night was black and full of wind and rain, but the shrill wind that snapped open and closed the doors and windows of Mark's cabin wasn't loud enough to drown out the sound of Abby talking smack at the television. Mark glanced at her, but he was more worried about the windows; they were the kind that opened outward like shutters, and most were whipping back and forth with enough force to make his teeth chatter. It had been like this all day, and now he gave the sky a worried glance from out of the largest window, then reached into the darkness and snatched at the frame, pulling it shut and latching it.

A futile gesture, Elektra thought as she watched from the wet darkness, and one that would never keep out the two figures she could see approaching the small building. She'd been waiting here since abandoning her spot on the ferry, and finally it was going to pay off—not ten feet away from her, one of them took a running start and then, in an incredible feat of athleticism, literally leaped onto the low roof. The other looked to the left and right, then melted back into his own little puddle of darkness.

Elektra watched a still blissfully ignorant Mark go from window to window, first securing them, then putting Xs of tape across each to keep them from shattering beneath the storm's force. Abby was in the living room and clearly visible through the X-marked window, seemingly transfixed in front of the television and focused on the Weather Channel's Storm Watch, waiting for word of the weather front that was battering the undersized island. Every fifteen or twenty seconds the picture digitized away in tiny blocks of coded signal, then it returned. With each brownout, Abby grew more impatient.

"I'm going to go get sandbags from the shed," her father told her.

Abby didn't look away from the television screen.

"Storm Watch," she sneered. "What a crock. They make it seem so exciting—tornado, hurricane, typhoon. Whatever—then it's just some stupid rain."

Mark grinned wryly and tossed her the roll of tape. "When your brain starts to rot?" he suggested. "Feel free to keep taping the windows."

Finally Abby turned away from the tube, ready to protest, but her father was already out the back door, pulling on his rain slicker as he went. So innocent, Elektra thought. He couldn't see the figure crouched on the roof directly above him, a man clad completely in the black garb of a *ninjutsu*. But to Elektra he was quite visible . . . as was the razor-sharp wire, a garotte, he was slowly lowering in front of Mark Miller's face.

Marked squinted at the shed across the muddy lawn, but he could barely see the tiny building through the rain pounding down. Taking a deep breath, he stepped forward.

He was barely an inch or two away from a sharp, hanging death when Elektra called out to him.

"Mark!"

He stopped, then turned back as he saw Elektra on the other side of the porch. His face registered his surprise at seeing her soaking wet figure.

"I need to talk to you," she yelled, fighting with the wind for volume. She gestured toward the door and moved toward it, and Mark obligingly followed suit, automatically stepping away from the almost invisible wire. Elektra could sense the ninja's surprise at seeing her, and his indecision. That indecision would kill him in another ten seconds.

"Can we go inside?" she shouted.

He cast a last look toward the shed, and Elektra could've sworn he looked relieved. No kidding—she wouldn't want to drag stuff out of there in this downpour either. "Yeah, sure."

She and Mark met at the back door at just about the same time, and she stood back while Mark twisted the knob and pushed inside. As soon as Mark's back was to her, Elektra silently slid out one of her sais, and, with a practiced and deadly flick of her wrist and a sharp, upward leap, she thrust the weapon through the underside of the porch roof. Alone on the porch for just a couple of seconds, she heard the smallest of death gasps, followed by a low *thump* as the ninja on the roof fell on his side and died. Her trained ear detected something else, too—a faint, evil hissing. Yeah, he was dead.

Inside, Mark was shrugging off his rain slicker and Abby was actually doing what her dad had suggested— going from window to window and taping them against breakage. She turned to see her father, then her startled gaze stopped on Elektra. "Hey," she said. "What's up?"

Elektra tried to figure out how to phrase this, but she couldn't. Finally, she said, "Abby, would you go into the bedroom for a minute? I need to talk to your dad."

Abby frowned and opened her mouth, but Mark held up a hand. "Go ahead, Ab. Now."

Abby rolled her eyes and mumbled something under her breath, but she reluctantly turned and headed for the other room. She went into the room, but stopped just beyond the door; she'd eavesdrop, but her dad knew there was nothing to be done about that.

Elektra nodded to herself. Somewhere outside was the other ninja—she could feel him—and by now he would know the fate of his partner, would have seen the green death mist rising from the body. There would be no mourning period, and the only thing this meant was that the remaining guy would be prepared to do the work of both men. That, Elektra knew, was going to be *big* trouble.

"Who are you?" Elektra demanded without preamble.

Mark blinked. "W-what?"

Elektra put her hands on her hips and took a step in his direction. "Mark, they won't just kill you, they'll kill Abby, too. So tell me right *now* who's after you and why."

For a moment, he was completely unable to speak, and he looked like a terrified baby rabbit trapped by a fox. His mouth worked as he tried to find a few words, but the only thing that came out was "Uh . . ." He took a step backward, trying to put some distance between him and Elektra—

Something cracked through the window and a silver dollar–sized hole appeared in the glass, right where his head had been only a half-second before.

"Dad!" Abby screamed. She charged out of the bedroom, aiming for her father, but Elektra literally swept the teenager off her feet, pivoted and shoved her into the small bathroom.

"Hey!" Mark protested. He tried to reach around her and grab Abby, but he missed. "You can't—"

Elektra didn't give him the chance to finish complaining. Hooking one foot in front of his ankle, she gave him a push; when he stumbled, he kept his momentum going and propelled himself into the bathroom after Abby, who was already trying to come out. He fell against her like a bowling ball and they both staggered back. "Stay there," Elektra commanded. "And stay *down*." She kicked the door shut and turned back to the living room, then paused for the barest of moments, just long enough to gather her concentration and blink her eyes closed—

Elektra sprinted for the front door, right before another hole crashed through the side window and a handful of six-inch razored compound bow bolts strafed across the living room. Glass exploded in every direction and bits of wood and plaster sailed through the air, pelting her in the face. The front door was almost within her reach when one of the bolts caught her square in the back, sinking deeply into the big trapezius muscle between her shoulder blades. She went down on her face, feeling fire course through her back as she tasted blood, but she still heard the front door shatter as the ninja outside kicked it in. He stepped through the splinters and saw her as she forced herself onto her elbows and rolled, landing on her back and bending the bolt's shaft sideways so that it ripped out a chunk of muscle and flesh. There was a noise, a sort of high-pitched keening, that she vaguely realized was coming from her own throat, and through foggy vision she saw the ninja whip out another arrow and load it into a Barnett Compound Crossbow. There was nothing she could do to stop or escape as he aimed and fired the bolt directly into her heart, then stepped over her body and went to look for Abby and Mark.

Elektra tilted her head and scowled toward the front door—clearly that was the wrong alternative. She squeezed her eyes shut again—

She spun and headed for the back door, just as the lone ninja leaped through the largest of the windows in the living room and fired directly into the spot where Elektra had just been standing. His bolts tore through the bathroom wall like it was made of paper. Most of them slammed into the mirror and sent pieces of spiked glass in all directions, but one found its target in the center of Mark's throat, killing him almost instantly. Abby screamed—

—the same way she did in Elektra's kimagure back on the ferry. So, the back door was also off the options list. She was running out of time here. She heard the door being kicked and tried one more time to concentrate, but she couldn't do it; whatever was going to happen was going down right *now*. When she refocused on the here and now, Elektra heard the front door shatter and found herself face-to-face with the remaining ninja. His compound bow was pointed directly at her chest, and before she could think of anything else, he fired.

Elektra let herself go fully into instinct.

She did a sharp backflip that an ordinary person would have found impossible. The burst of arrows skimmed over her and, except for the one she literally caught in midair, the rest burst through the wall behind her, disintegrating the skimpy barrier between the bathroom and living area. They hammered into the mirror and it shattered, making Abby scream. Her father reached for her but missed as she flung open the bathroom door—

"Abby, *no!*"

—then froze as the scene before her registered in her brain. Her gaze took in everything, as it always did: Elektra, still tumbling in the air with one of the arrows clutched in her hand, the room full of projectiles, the black-clad ninja with his finger releasing the trigger as the last bolt shot from his canister.

Elektra's vision skipped around the room as she turned, over and over and over again. One, two—

"Thirteen arrows."

Her whisper was lost in the sound of the bow's firing. Elektra landed in a crouch as the last one whizzed past her shoulder and the ninja ejected the smoking bolt canister from his compound bow. It rolled across the floor as he jerked a fresh one from his belt—

She sprang.

Thunk!

The ninja's eyes went wide with pain as Elektra embedded the arrow deep into his left shoulder, paralyzing his arm. His hand fell to the floor, palm up and useless as the full load of ammunition spun away. Then his eyes narrowed and he snarled at her.

"Abby—Jesus!" Mark cried. He grabbed his daughter and tried to pull her back into the nonexistent safety of the bathroom. The ninja threw a stiff-fingered punch at Elektra that would have broken her cheekbone had she been stupid enough to let it connect; instead she ducked under it, then sent a vicious punch straight into the man's solar plexus. When he doubled over, she pinned his calf in place, then dropped her full body weight on his knee; it shattered with enough force to where both Abby and Mark heard the bone disintegrate. The ninja gasped, but to his credit, he still didn't scream.

He also still didn't go down.

He careened backward on one leg, falling against the opposite wall and sliding down it at the same time he ripped a set of throwing stars off his belt. With a speed that was still like lightning, he brought his hand up—

One of Elektra's sais pierced the ninja's palm and nailed it brutally to the floor.

Elektra could hear Mark's astonished intake of breath, but right now she couldn't take the time to be concerned about how shocked he and Abby were at seeing someone they'd thought was an ordinary woman leave a professional killer bloody, broken, and paralyzed. There were things she needed to know, and she *would* get this information.

She crouched over the ninja and pressed the tip of her other sai to his temple. The skin indented and broke just enough to ooze a single drop of scarlet.

"Who sent you?" she snapped. *"Dare ga o mae wo okurikonda?"* When he didn't answer, she used her other hand to rip the black mask free of his face, but there was nothing special about the thin Japanese man smiling benignly up at her. Well, if you discounted the fact that he *could* still smile given the amount of pain he had to be in.

"In a moment, you will know," he said. *"Sugu, omae ni wakaru hazusa."* His black eyes gleamed, then he turned his head as far to the left as he could, straining the muscles in his neck until they stood out like ropes.

Elektra pulled the sai back reflexively. "No!"

But the sai, as it turned out, wasn't even needed. The ninja saw to his own death by snapping his head back in the other direction so hard . . .

. . . that he broke his own neck.

126

Elektra scrambled to her feet and backed away, vaguely aware of Abby gagging behind her. When she glanced over, even Mark looked green around the edges and decidedly shaky, but there was no time for that now. There was more to come, and if she or the other two got in the way, they'd join this guy in whatever realm he now wandered.

"Get back!" she hissed at them.

There was the sudden smell of sulfur, like a thousand matches being lit at once, then acrid green smoke began pouring from beneath the dead man's clothes. It was vile and thick, and while Elektra had never seen nuclear waste vapor, she imagined this was what it would look like. They were *out* of time.

"Get back *now!*" she screamed, and leaped at Abby and Mark. Her grab pulled the two of them into a tumble with her that Elektra kept going until they were all crushed against the far wall. At the last second, she yanked the pitiful remains of the bathroom door down and in front of them, using it as a last-ditch shield.

Whoosh!

The green smoke suddenly boiled into white-hot flame. It pulsed outward, sending a ripple of horrible heat in their direction. They huddled behind the door as the front of it blistered and peeled and almost caught fire itself.

Finally, it was over. Elektra stepped boldly out, but Mark and Abby followed more carefully, their faces still tinged with fear. The ninja's smoldering remains were in the living room, and for all the whiteness of the fire that had consumed him, the flames and the destruction of his body had left an ugly, telltale black circle on the ceiling above him. Mark looked from the Ninja's corpse to Abby and back again, before finally turning to face Elektra.

She knew he probably had a thousand questions, but all that really mattered right now was that Abby was safe and he was still alive and in good enough shape to take care of her.

With a little help.

"We have to go," Elektra said flatly. "There'll be more of them coming."

Mark dug a hand into his unruly hair and tugged, an odd little gesture that Elektra understood at once— there was nothing like a good stinging on your scalp to convince you that you weren't having a nightmare, that you actually *were* experiencing something.

Without another word, the three of them ran into the night and piled into Mark's truck.

10

SAN PEDRO, CALIFORNIA

STONE WAS STEPPING AWAY FROM HIS CORNER AND headed into a cage fight when he got the message from Kirigi.

It wasn't much, just a little blip on the color screen of his cell phone that the guy managing his corner, who was more of a figurehead than anything else, held up for Stone to interpret because he had no idea what it meant. But Stone knew, all right, and it made him grin evilly to see it; Kirigi wanted him, which meant the Master had something special in mind, and it had to be something big to call Kirigi all the way over to Japan. Usually Kirigi wasn't much on telephones—he was traditional Japan and liked the old ways, at least most of the time—but even he had to admit that nothing spelled instant communication like the modern-day cell phone. At other times, Kirigi kind of reminded Stone of an impatient gangbanger, some bad-ass dude right out of Chinatown who was just aching to fight his way to the top of the street hierarchy, even if he had to use his bare hands. Stone might have invulnerability, but Kirigi had a lot of mystical monkey business on his side, and Stone knew better than to mess with the man.

Stone went into the cage with the roar of the crowd ringing in his ears, although Stone knew that the cheering wasn't for him. The cage itself was octagonal, and was just about as big as a good-sized living room. The floor was covered by a gray mat that had been crudely repaired in at least a dozen places. The mat had some really ugly stains on it, old and brown, and their origin was obvious. By the looks of it, the stitched-up patches might have been put there by any one of the longshoremen sitting in the stands; bets were being made and money was changing hands fast among the tough-looking men and women out there whose faces evidenced dozens of nationalities.

His opponent was clearly the favorite in tonight's match, a local California boy on his way to going pro fighter because the Hollywood scene had turned out to be less than kind despite his pretty-boy face. Like a hundred thousand others, the boy had found out there was more to the movies than muscles and mouth; he needed talent, too, and in that he was sadly lacking. Stone had barely paid attention to all the prefight hype (although there'd been plenty)—he seldom did, since he was just in it for the bloodshed and fun—but he *did* recall this one's name: Gunny Breeze. According to circuit rumor, the name had been given to the kid by his old man, a cantankerous retired Marine turned fight coach. Anyone who looked at the elder Breeze could tell he was he was a career hard case and twice as mean as a snake; the kid was doing well in the matches because he was supposed to be just like his dad.

There was a certain atmosphere in an ultimate fighting arena, one that was very different from a regular martial arts or boxing match. Yeah, there was the usual noise and screaming for the favorites, but underneath that was a vague sense of . . . *primitiveness*, of mankind dropped back thousands of years and embracing its Stone Age roots. The cage itself fed the undercurrent of danger—bigger than a boxing ring, completely enclosed by metal, it offered no escape to the two men inside it. It was possible—always—that someone could die within that aluminum chain-link fencing. The combatants knew this, and the audience did, too . . . and they wanted it. They *all* wanted it.

Breeze was a big guy, nearly as muscular as Stone himself . . . but any comparison ended there. Breeze was blond and blue-eyed where Stone's skin was the color of coffee, and his eyes were black as a puddle of oil. Even though Stone knew the boy didn't stand a chance, he had to admire him—there was none of the misplaced self-confidence he'd so often encountered on the ultimate fighting circuit, where too many men had looked at Stone and assumed his size meant slowness and too much body fat. Gunny Breeze's gaze was cold and calculating—this boy was a killer just waiting to be trained. Stone liked that . . . but he also needed to get this over with so he could get on a flight to Japan.

The cage door closed around the two fighters and the referee. The crowd screamed in anticipation, pressing as close to the fencing as they could, the braver ones trying for a better look and risking a crack on the side of the head or a shove backward by one of the burly bouncers to get it. Stone and Gunny studied each other warily, although Stone was playing into it more to give the crowd a decent show than anything else. When the bell went off, the ref, a balding, slightly overweight man in his forties, wisely got the hell out of the way and the two huge fighters went for each other.

The boy wasn't a lightweight, but Stone figured he could still take Gunny out with a couple of punches, especially if he landed one in the face. Gunny would be faster, but everybody in the place knew that Stone had the real power—one look at his arms was an indicator of how much damage he'd do if he connected. But there was still that *if* factor; Gunny wasn't going to go the boxing route if he could help it—he was way too smart for that. Instead, he came in low and light on his feet, ducked under Stone's tight right hook (the one that surprised almost everyone), dropped hard onto his left hip, and swept Stone's legs out from under him.

Stone went down with a grunt and he could've sworn he heard the concrete somewhere beneath the thick matting actually *crack*. He stayed there for a few moments, actually *waiting* for Gunny to come after him until the ref hurried up and started to evaluate him. That wasn't an option, but apparently neither was Breeze coming after him, either—the kid was going to wait until he got back to his feet. Stone rolled to his side and levered himself upward, waving away the referee and eyeing his opponent with a higher level of respect. Gunny wasn't stupid enough to box with Stone, but he wasn't about to go to ground with him, either. The kid must've taken one look at Stone's massive neck and decided nothing short of King Kong—which he wasn't—was going to be able to get a choke hold on that.

Stone licked his lips and hunkered down a little more, bending his knees and spreading his fingers wide. He thought he was ready for the attack, but when it came, the boy took him completely by surprise when instead of repeating his first takedown, he went after Stone as if Stone was the bowling ball and he was the pin. Stone found himself on the ground for the second time, and now he was starting to feel humiliated in addition to being rushed. Kirigi didn't like to wait, and by now his Master had a jet being primed on the runway at John Wayne Airport in Santa Ana. It was even more of a struggle to get himself upright this time—a man who weighed as much as he did didn't fall lightly, and he didn't get back up that way either.

Gunny still wasn't coming after him, but the guy did look just a shade more pleased with himself about the situation. That was annoying but not the end of the world; he might have knocked Stone down a couple of times, but there was going to be a whole lot more on Gunny's to-do list if he still thought he was going to get the better of Stone.

His next attempt at a takedown proved just that.

His problem was pretty obvious: while he still had a healthy respect for Stone's size and strength, the two previous takedowns had made him think his opponent was slow and easy prey for putting off balance. With this thought in mind, the boy decided that to please the crowd, he should get a little fancier, and a flying scissor kick would be just the ticket for upping the cheering factor.

It wasn't so much overconfidence as a serious miscalculation. Breeze had thought he had enough body weight behind him to pull it off, but the simple fact was that he didn't—Stone outweighed him by nearly sixty pounds, and by the time Breeze thought he was going to make Stone hit the mat a third time, Stone was as firmly planted on that mat as a hundred-year-old oak tree. He did go down . . . but only because he wanted to. And then he did it a whole lot faster than Gunny Breeze had been counting on.

Breeze came in with a picture-perfect elbow grab—Stone gave it to him—then levered his body up with one leg in front of Stone's thighs and the other behind them. Stone let himself be guided toward the ground, and he felt the kid's surprise at how easy it was; a split second later Stone also sensed when that surprise turned to dismay as Stone suddenly increased his downward speed. He landed solidly on Breeze's right leg and pinned him there, and before the guy could get his left leg bent up to push himself away, Stone had that one pinned, too. Breeze bent at the waist and brought himself up only to take a hard backfist that was clearly more of an annoyance punch than anything serious on Stone's part. By then the ref was standing over them to take a look, and as a result, little surfer boy suddenly went all frantic. After all, his title was on the line, and he wasn't going to lose it so easily—and certainly *not* in the first round—to an oversized ape of an outsider who'd gotten in on the fights via a last-minute sign-up ticket. The ref wasn't going to call him out just because he was trapped, so Breeze, feeling like he was still up on energy and good at his game, put everything he had into twisting his body and making an escape.

He must not have thought Stone was as heavy as he was, or maybe he just assumed that if he put enough effort into it, Stone would let go.

Stone didn't.

The kid jerked beneath him and Stone's body vibrated with the effort Breeze put into it—it felt like there was a huge snake beneath him that was trying to squeeze through a hole the size of a bottle cap. Stone easily held his ground as the boy forced his body around. One second Stone was just lying there and Breeze was turning his legs underneath Stone's; the next, a noise filled the air, something that sounded like a piece of porcelain breaking in two.

Then Breeze started screaming.

Stone looked down, but he wasn't surprised at what he saw. The boy definitely had determination, and sometimes, in cases like these, that stubbornness could cause disastrous results. Breeze had, indeed, managed to get his body to turn—

—but his right foot hadn't turned with it.

The ref rushed over and began gesturing wildly— "*He's out! He's out!*"—but it still took Stone a good six seconds to get his weight off the boy. Maybe he could have gone a little faster—all right, he definitely *could* have—but Stone had gone from being impressed with Breeze to being annoyed at his foolishness. Even so, the California kid was lucky. Stone could have killed him at any time during this match as easily as he blinked.

He watched impassively as the cage door was jerked open and a doctor ran in, followed by the kid's corner man, then three or four other people. They left Breeze where he was, and it was a while before the doc slipped him a shot that at least got him to stop that raw screaming. Stone was the winner, of course, but he shocked the crowd and his corner man by just getting up and walking out—never mind the victory words or the trophy, and they could mail the prize money to his post office box.

Kirigi needed him.

ZIMBABWE, AFRICA

This place was soaked in death.

The unpaved streets—if they could be called that—were wide and dusty, disused. Even the trash that pressed up against the sad and sorry-looking buildings bore a coat of African dirt that obliterated its origin. Too far away from Gwanda—itself so small it had little impact on anything—to be remembered and too small to be noticed by the press, this place was like a pocket of lost life buried in the countryside. It had its own tiny government, but there were no people of power in charge; the few men who ran it had, sadly, made choices in the past that had aligned them with those whose existence would now ultimately help fuel its destruction and destroy them. Circumstance had made it into a dry and colorless sort of nonplace, so beaten down with hunger, poverty, and sickness that few of its own people even recalled its name . . . and no one at all actually cared.

Typhoid Mary walked through the village slowly, not touching anything—yet—but looking at everything and everyone; then she turned and walked back again. The famine here had played no favorites and its victims were everywhere, although, of course, it had sucked away the lives of the youngest and oldest first. Like a lioness singling out her prey, the hunger had honed in on those too old and week to fight its effects, melting away their will along with their body fat and immune systems.

Yes, this would be the perfect place for her next game.

What was left now was small, its original population of over three hundred reduced by a more than fifty percent death toll and others who had fled, looking for life in places other than the marked-for-doom village they had once called home. The deaths in the larger cities made the news regularly, but nothing places like this were routinely missed—after all, who thought about a nowhere village where the fanciest building was a two-room shack with a decrepit straw grass roof? That dwelling belonged to the village chief, whose children still lived, although not very well. His pleas for help to the military had gone unheard because of his people's previous affiliation with the party opposing the president; now it was as if they didn't exist. If they *did* receive supplies—a rare occasion, indeed—it was items that no one else wanted or his workers found that the food was so old that half of it had already rotted within the packaging.

The adults saw her, but it was the children who most interested Typhoid.

She had always been partial to them, with their sweet and innocent faces, their big, pleading eyes. She loved it when their faces turned upward and stared at her and their eyes filled with tears. Not that she could do anything about it—not that she *would*—but she reveled in the helplessness and the pain, even if it wasn't caused by her. So many people didn't appreciate the true value of suffering—without suffering, how could a person ever truly appreciate being alive in the first place? How could he or she know the beauty of no pain if there had been no experience, no true *immersion*, in agony? People took such things for granted and they fought pain with every ounce of strength that they had; instead, they should have welcomed it, sought it out, and lived with it, day by day. To be without pain was to be without sensation, without feeling, and there was no wisdom in an existence like that.

And these children . . . they were so much more mature than adults in the matters of pain. They bore it silently and without complaint, never crying or whining, saving every bit of their energy so they could fight for life for another day, another hour, another five minutes. And every single one of them gave to someone else—they shared the tiny bits of food they had, they shared what comfort they could, they shared *themselves*.

Just as Typhoid would share of herself.

They were drawn to her. She was the beautiful Asian

woman among the mass of dark-skinned adults and children, quietly drifting among them like a golden-tinted ghost. They were the walking nearly dead—naked skeletal bodies with bloated bellies, huge, hairless skulls with tiny, glittering teeth and sunken eyes. Her sparkling, sympathetic gaze invited them to come forward and touch her. They begged for food, and she gave out pieces of candy crawling with her death; they wanted to touch the silk fabric of her blouse and slacks, so she invited one after another to crawl onto her lap and be hugged; they wanted comfort, so she pressed her black lips against the dried-out skin of their scalps, giving dozens of them little kisses of disease. In death she would give them freedom, finally, from their suffering. Yes, this was a good place, a very special place, but . . .

Kirigi was calling to her.

Typhoid felt his need the instant it sang through her blood. He wanted her for something, something important, and his silent call was like fuel to her addiction. Like her beloved pain, Kirigi was a *sensation* in her veins, the cry of a drug only she used and which she could not deny.

With a final goodbye kiss to the people who watched her, blown on the dark wind of an isolated forest, Typhoid Mary drifted out of the village she'd ensured would never survive and headed back to Japan.

There were people who lived on this primitive trop-ical island, but those who did built their crude wooden homes on stilts and pulled what little livestock they had inside at night. They farmed the rocky soil but not very successfully, and they catered to the tourists who came with the diving and biking companies, welcom-ing the foreign money to help support themselves in their poor economy. They left the tourists to make their way, safely or not, with the guides, but the native islanders watched their own children constantly and even the adults stayed in pairs and traveled armed with heavy walking sticks and machetes, although speed was always the best defense.

If you couldn't outrun the dragons, you couldn't sur-vive.

Tattoo grinned and followed behind the guide he'd hired to lead him into the denser jungle on Pulau Komodo. The brown-skinned man, whose name was Budi, knew the trails well, and Tattoo had to stay on his toes to keep up. Budi was a local guy, older and balding, with black eyes and skin as sun-wrinkled as an old belt; he'd looked at Tattoo critically and decided he was good to go physically. Pressing a crumpled American twenty-dollar bill into Budi's hand—enough money to support his impoverished family for at least a month—

had ensured the guy would take Tattoo to see what he wanted.

It was hot and humid here, and Budi had told him in broken English that November, only a month ago, had actually been the hottest month of the year. There were plenty of dragons around, but they were slow and sluggish because of the humidity, with less of a tendency to be aggressive; this obviously made it a good time to visit and study them. Tattoo was very interested in these prehistoric animals, and while the guide could think he was a tree-hugger environmentalist or a misguided animal lover, Tattoo had his own reasons for wanting to get close to them. It all had to do with that long, blank patch of skin on the outside length of his left leg.

Picking his way up a steep, rocky slope in front of Tattoo, the guide came to the crest of it and stopped, then gestured back at his tourist. *"Ora,"* Budi said, pointing. *"Buaja darat."* Ora was the local word for Komodo dragon, and Tattoo had heard the term often since his arrival. The other phrase meant "land crocodile," something Budi was using only, he thought, to impress this man who he thought was nothing but an ignorant tourist. The dragons were really lizards that could grow huge, up to ten feet long and three hundred pounds, with bacteria-drenched mouths that gave infectious bites to their prey. They were fast runners and surprise attackers, cannibalistic to their own young, and the island's visitors and guides did well to stay out of their way. It had taken a bit of doing to find this guide, who was willing to get Tattoo closer to the lizards than anyone else, but *not* in the context of the more sluggish, people-accustomed ones that hung around the rangers' shacks. No, Tattoo needed to see them in the wild, in *action*—he wanted to see them at rest, and he wanted to see them attack and feed. As magnificent as the animal might be, he needed to make sure it was worthy and . . . *capable* of being added to his body.

Tattoo moved up beside Budi and stared down the slope. Sunning itself on a large, flat rock not twenty feet below them was an impressively sized lizard. It was difficult to estimate, but Tattoo would guess the creature was close to two hundred fifty pounds, easily twice the weight of the light-framed Budi. This was exactly what he was looking for; now Tattoo needed only to watch the creature feed.

He could hear the high whine of the insects in the trees behind him, but they were too far away from the shore to hear the waves. Everything was lush and green and, except for their own breathing and the bugs, nearly church quiet. The noxious smell of the fat lizard drifted up to them on the wind, and Tattoo saw it flick its long, yellow tongue out a couple of times as it tasted the air. It did it again, then cocked its big head and swung it in their direction, searching for their smell.

After all, in the world of the *Ora*, humans were just one more type of meat.

Pleased, Tattoo turned to look at Budi, but the man had already raised his defenses to the ready; he had backed a few feet away and his dark face had gone suspicious and . . . *hungry*. It was a look with which Tattoo was familiar many times over, and it scared him not in the least. In Budi's right hand was a dirty-looking knife about four inches long that he must have pulled from a belt sheath hidden inside the waist of his loose linen pants. It was Tattoo's American money that had prompted this decision, of course—Budi knew there was more in Tattoo's pockets, and greed was always the greatest source of false courage in a foreign country.

"*Uang*," Budi demanded roughly.

Tattoo knew what the word meant—money—but he still played stupid, only frowning and shaking his hand. "I don't understand," he said with as much wide-eyed innocense as he could manage.

Budi wasn't fooled. He gestured impatiently at Tattoo's pockets. "*Uang!*" he said again, louder, and this time he made a cutting gesture with the blade. Only a fool wouldn't understand, and few tourists were *that* dumb. "Give to me!"

" 'Give to me,' " Tattoo mimicked with a sneer. He raised one eyebrow but made no move to comply. "The least you could do is use the English word for what you think you're going to steal." Budi stared at him in amazement and Tattoo continued. "It's *money*, remember? *Mo-ney*. I'd tell you to practice getting the accent on the correct syllable, but you're not going to need it anymore, so why bother?"

Budi scowled at him, and Tattoo guessed the man had understood very little of what he'd been told. A shame, because he wasn't going to live much longer and a man had a right to comprehend his last conversation. "Give to me," Budi repeated, and this time he punctuated his sentence with a jab of the knife in Tattoo's direction. There was too much distance between them for Tattoo to be intimidated, but this routine had probably worked for Budi before. Tattoo could easily picture it: trusting tourists, the greedy tour guide—Budi would threaten them with the knife, then take their money and leave them to find their own way back to the ranger's station. They might make it, they might not—Komodo dragons weren't the least bit afraid of humans and it wasn't hard to imagine one running down a full-grown man. One bite and a couple of hours of patience on the lizard's part would do it; the guy would quickly become too sick and weak to run. Often several other lizards would join in and tear the prey apart, fighting for their share of a free meal.

Speaking of Komodo dragons, the one on the rocks below had shifted its position, moving a cautious half dozen feet in their direction. It must be hungry. Excellent.

Budi found a little bravado and took a couple of steps toward Tattoo, waving his knife menacingly in the air between them. Even so, the only thing Tattoo was worried about was that the thing looked so filthy. He couldn't recall the last time he'd had a tetanus shot.

"*Sekarang!*"

Tattoo's Indonesian was pretty rudimentary, but he recognized the word for *now*. He shrugged and began calmly unbuttoning his shirt. Budi watched with a puzzled expression but he didn't say anything; maybe he thought Tattoo had a money belt across his chest—the American tourists were known to hide things on their bodies. But what Tattoo had across his skin was a whole lot more problematic than a tourist money holder.

Tattoo's shirt was a loose-fitting garment with three-quarter length sleeves, the kind common among plantation owners in Cuba—light, breezy, but with plenty of gauzy material for protection from the hot sun. The last couple of buttons were tucked into his jeans so Tattoo left these alone and simply shrugged the upper part of the fabric down, letting it slide off his shoulders and drape around his waist as he pulled his arms free.

Budi blinked and stared at Tattoo's chest, then he recovered and grinned. "*Mungil*," he said and pointed, then frowned as he tried to figure out the appropriate wording. "Cute, yes. But you give . . . *money* to me *sekarang*."

Tattoo nodded, then folded his arms across his chest

as if he were hugging himself and closed his eyes so he could concentrate, just for a moment. With his hands comfortably beneath his own arms, he felt first the bulge, then the soft skins of the two creatures he wanted as they pulled free of his flesh and nestled into his palms. Even though they wouldn't bite him, the tips of their tiny teeth felt like needles scraping against his fingers. His oversensitive hearing picked up a small sound and he opened his eyes to a slit; out of the corner of one of them, Tattoo saw that the Komodo dragon had worked its way a little farther up the slope; now it was only about ten feet away. For an animal that was said to be able to run as fast as a dog, less than three yards' distance wasn't much at all. Budi gave it a nervous glance, but circumstances now dictated that he must keep an eye on the white man he was robbing.

"I am waiting no more," Budi announced. He shot another quick glance at the lizard. *"Sekarang* I cut you."

Tattoo nodded, as if he were in total acceptance of his fate at Budi's hands. Then he unfolded his arms and spread the fingers of both his hands as wide as he could.

The two vampire bats rocketed upward, making Budi jerk in surprise. But the best was yet to come: the bats went only about fifteen feet toward the sky before they reversed direction and spiraled back down . . . then went straight for Budi's eyes.

The guide screamed and flailed at the air with his knife, but it was a useless defense—the bats were much too small, fast, and vicious. He swiped at the air, then hit himself in the head as he tried to get one off him; blood streamed down his face as it bit into the tender skin just above his eyelid. "*Jahat! Jahat!*"

Tattoo grinned as he recognized the word for devil amid a stream of other indecipherable words, then he backed up a couple of feet when Budi twisted, then tripped over a small boulder and fell. Pebbles bounced in all directions, skittering down and pelting the attentive Komodo dragon. The sharp-edged rocks along the crest of the slope cut Budi in a dozen places as he cried out—"*Bantu!*"—now trying to get Tattoo to help him. But Tattoo had no intention of doing any such thing; in fact, he was just waiting for the inevitable.

And so was the dragon.

His two bats twisted back up, then dove again; this time one of them hit pay dirt, and the intensity of Budi's screams changed, turning raw as one of the creatures' teeth dug deep into the meat of his right eye. Blood, abundant and shockingly bright in this green universe, spit from between the fingers of the hand that Budi slapped over his eye; with his other he swiped awkwardly at the bat that was still fluttering around his face, reaching out reflexively to try and grab it; abruptly his cries of pain turned into a bellow of dismay as he tumbled down the other side of the rock-strewn slope. Budi bounced and rolled, knocking painfully against too many rocks to count. When he finally came to a stop, his scalp was crimson with blood and bruised, split skin, that one eye had been gouged out, and who knew how many broken bones he had.

For a long moment, Budi was silent. And when he finally opened his remaining eye, his groan of agony turned to a death scream as he saw the Komodo dragon's mouth yawn wide and its teeth closed over his head.

Tattoo stood on the upper slope and watched silently as his bats returned to roost and worked their way carefully into the skin just below his shoulder blades, one on each side. Yes, with the proper ceremony and given the painstaking process of infusing the ink onto his skin, the Komodo dragon would be a wonderful and proud addition to his arsenal of shadow animals. For now, however, he must leave the voracious creature to its meal, trusting in the eyes of the hawk that yanked its way free of his upper arm to show him the way out of the jungle.

Kirigi was calling him.

11

TOKYO, JAPAN

THIS TIME, ROSHI'S CONFERENCE ROOM WAS already full.

The *ikuren* had come at his beckoning, all those men of power scuttling from the corners of the huge city like oversized cockroaches simply because he had decreed they should. They were expensively dressed in designer suits and Italian shoes and sporting three-hundred-dollar haircuts. But like the Asian gangsters they originally were and would always remain, their lined and knowing faces betrayed lifetimes of street savvy and hard knocks. Their hooded eyes flicked left to right, mistrustful of each other, predictable only in that to another man's face they would be polite . . . but they would always be calculating and *hungry*.

As usual, Meizumi sat to the right of Roshi's chair. He was Roshi's key man and the only one who knew Roshi's every move . . . or at least he liked to think so. Even so, he had notions about the truth—a man like

Roshi must always have his secrets, lest he inadvertently reveal his weaknesses, too.

And here, at last, came the newest of the players in Roshi's never-ending game.

Stone was an enormous man who looked like a black Sumo wrestler. Dressed in a long black leather vest, leather slacks, and black leather boots, his head was shaven clean except for a square patch on the back of his scalp; that part was long and pulled into a heavy, black braid. His arms were bigger than most men's thighs, and his neck was lost in the huge knots of muscle along his shoulders. Stone was a frightening figure and he knew it. He also knew that now was not the place to be overbearing, but for all of his bulk and his attempts to step quietly, it was obvious he had no clue that every step he took made the floor and walls vibrate—he looked like a walking mountain.

Not far behind was another young black man named Kinkou, a street punk dressed completely in ragged black pants and a sleeveless T-shirt covered with Japanese writing. His slender frame was corded with muscle, and his face was unreadable; the only thing that seemed to please him was that he could balance a coin on the tip of one finger.

Tattoo followed, and to those in attendance he was a strange sight, indeed. He was dressed here, of course, but everyone in the room knew that beneath his clothing the long-haired man was completely covered in animal tattoos, the most prominent of which was a hawk whose eyes shifted and examined everyone who passed. He hid his ink beneath the black fabric and finished it off with a floor-length black coat.

Trailing behind Tattoo was Typhoid Mary, an exquisitely sensual young woman wearing a kimono, whose face was made up in the porcelain white mask of an actress in a Noh play. Black kohl outlined her eyes and lips, and when she took a seat, those closest to her intentionally shifted their chairs to put distance between themselves and her.

And finally, Kirigi. For this meeting, the tall and handsome young man had donned the traditional robes, a cream-colored set sporting dragons sewn in scarlet thread across both sides of the front. Perhaps he dressed formally as a counterbalance to the fact that he was the youngest of the ikuren and considered to be the most reactionary, a trait not especially prized. Even so, he had the easy confidence and good humor of an aristocrat, and the ego to go with it. His mouth smiled lightly above eyes that were constantly seeking and measuring everyone else in the room.

Only the empty chair at the head of the table remained: *Roshi's*.

The elder entered the board room and took his seat with quiet grace, then waited while everyone else finished with their respectful bows, settled back down, and gave him their full attention. "I believe," he said, "that Kirigi wishes to address the council."

With a nod of acquiescence toward Roshi, Kirigi stood, then scanned the other people in the room while that same enigmatic half-smile played across his lips. Murmurs ripped through the board members— even to those who made killing their livelihood, Kirigi was considered charismatic and intimidating, unpredictable. There was no guessing as to what he might do next.

Kirigi finally turned back to face Roshi, then bowed again. "Venerable Master," he said in a deferential tone, "I fear that we are unworthy of you."

Roshi said nothing, but the tiniest raising of one black eyebrow let Kirigi and the others know that neither he nor the rest of the men believed Kirigi's pseudo-apology.

Kirigi lowered his gaze so that he was not meeting Roshi's. "Despite our delicacy and subtlety," he continued, "we have failed to resolve the problem of the treasure."

A nervous ripple went through the room. No one was fooled by the careful wording—this was nothing but an insult presented in diplomatic terms. But decades of leadership had taught Roshi how to be just that, and his face maintained a bland, unreadable smile.

Meizumi, however, would not take this humiliation without defending his leader and himself. His expression twisted in anger. "Roshi gave that task to *me*," he said indignantly.

"Yes," Kirigi said in an oily voice. "Exactly."

Meizumi's face went red. "And my men are taking care of it." He was trying to keep his tone level, but his anger was starting to bleed through. He was struggling to hide it, knowing that not being able to disguise his feelings would be considered a weakness.

Kirigi swiveled his head and caught Meizumi in his black, bottomless gaze. "Your men are dead." He said it as if he were relating some boring bit of weather-related information.

Meizumi's mouth dropped open, but no sound came out. He looked at once outraged and shocked, as if he was convinced Kirigi was lying but didn't know how to prove it.

But Roshi's next statement confirmed the worst. "Killed by the female assassin," he said. "The gaijin, Elektra." The leader's words were matter-of-fact, but there was a hint of sympathy in them for the man who had, until now, been his second-in-command.

Without changing his expression, Kirigi extended his hand to the right, and Kinkou reached beneath the table to retrieve something, which he then transferred to Kirigi's palm. Kirigi leaned over and carefully put it directly in front of Meizumi.

Meizumi looked down at the *tanto*, a blade without a hilt that had been wrapped in several sheets of paper to provide him with a good grip. Beneath his black hair, his skin had gone impossibly white, like bone bleached by a desert sun. He swallowed and glanced at the other men, but they were avoiding his gaze; when he looked to Roshi, his mentor's face was impassive, his eyes knowing. There were no alternatives.

Swallowing again, Meizumi pushed back his chair and stood. At the same time, a ghostlike servant pulled open a door at the end of the room, and when Meizumi looked in that direction, he finally understood that this was really happening. Not only did his beloved Roshi expect him to commit *seppuku* for failing in his duties, but he had already appointed a *kaishakunin*—assistant—and prepared the *chado*. The *kaishakunin*, who was waiting patiently with a white *kamishimo* for Meizumi draped over one arm, would take him through the proper tea ceremony and ritual and, if necessary, provide the killing blow should Meizumi not be able to do so. Through the open door, Meizumi could see the unlacquered wooden table—the *sanbo*—and the sake, pen, and *washi* placed upon it—how ironic that he would be required to carry his own *kozuka* into the room. Would he be able to write a good death poem, or would Roshi read it later and shake his head in disgust? He hoped he would make his mentor proud.

Meizumi did not look back at the others as he reverentially picked up the *tanto* and carried it to the waiting *kaishakunin*. The other man silently ushered him inside the small room and quietly closed the door behind him.

No one said anything for a long time, and no doubt each *ikuren* had plenty to think about in the silence. It was to Meizumi's honor that he did not change his mind or begin screaming in cowardice, that he had accepted his fate in a manly and courageous manner.

Finally, Kirigi spoke. "Master Roshi, I humbly request that you allow me this task. Perhaps with a little less delicacy, my forces will not be defeated by a mere assassin."

Roshi sat back and contemplated this, his gaze faraway and pinned to the closed door. Kirigi remained standing and kept his silence—he knew what the master was waiting for. Another few minutes and they all heard it: Meizumi's muffled death grunt. There was no sound of falling, so the assistant had known the ritual well enough to ensure that Meizumi had tucked his *kamishimo* sleeves under his knees, taking care that Meizumi did not end his seppuku in an undignified tumble or slump to one side. It was over.

"It is yours, Kirigi," Roshi said, pulling everyone's attention back to himself. "Complete it, and you will have proven yourself worthy of leading this council. I will step aside."

The other ikuren gaped at Roshi, but Kirigi and his group were pleased. They stood, bowed, and filed out without saying anything else, ignoring the stares and the scowls, their faces shining with anticipation. Only Typhoid turned before stepping out the door; she gave a dark smile to the glowering man closest to her, then blew him a kiss. His frown deepened, but a moment later it turned into a cough, heavy, wet, and deep in his chest as though he had a sudden, vicious case of the flu.

The instant the last of Kirigi's crew had left, one of the more senior board members jumped to his feet to voice his objections. "But sir, his methods will destroy us. It—"

Roshi held up a hand, instantly silencing him, then motioned for the man to retake his seat. "Perhaps Kirigi is right. Perhaps it is time for a new direction." Having said that, he turned his back and walked out, leaving them to speculate and complain among themselves. By their expressions of frustration and disbelief, most of them obviously already thought he was blind, but his decisions were not for them to question. Most of them were too short-sighted for competent decision making anyway; that was why *he* was the leader, and not one of them.

He sent a brief, sideways glance at the trickle of blood seeping from beneath the doorway of the closed room, then slowly made his way to his garden to meditate.

Well, Elektra thought, it's early morning and at least we're all still alive. For a few moments last night, she'd had her doubts about making that happen. Now, sitting on the passenger side of Mark's truck with Abby in the middle, she didn't feel much better about their situation even though Mark was pulling the truck into an empty spot on the outbound ferry. How had she gotten herself into this predicament? What was it about Mark and Abby that had triggered the *No Way* switch inside her heart, the one that said she'd had enough of the killing—at least for now—and she was going to flipside this job and keep them *alive*? She had no idea, but there was no going back now. They'd be lucky if the Hand didn't send the whole world after them.

As soon as they'd cut the motor to the truck and the ferry had pulled away from the dock, Elektra found a spot on the deck that was a little apart from the rest of the passengers and began punching numbers into her cell phone. It took a number of tries, but she finally got McCabe on the phone; he would—maybe—give her the information she sought.

"The Hand—ninjas, of all people." McCabe's voice was tinny with distance, but Elektra could still make out the note of amazement in it. *"This is serious, Elektra. Who's going to help you with that?"*

"Where is he?" she demanded in a low voice. She tried placing her hand over the mouthpiece for privacy, but that didn't work; it just muffled her words and then McCabe couldn't hear her. Anyone could be on this ferry, and the water and the wind had a nasty way of carrying a person's conversation to ears that shouldn't be hearing it, and she was having a frustrating time. "Just get me a *location!*"

She listened to McCabe talking, pressing the cell phone into her ear in an effort to block out the noise around her. Finally she snapped the telephone shut and glared at the grayness above the water as if she could make it go away. "Damn it," she muttered, a little too loudly.

The back of her neck tickled a warning, and when she turned, Elektra grimaced when she saw Abby looking at her with a reproachful expression. She didn't have to hear the *Don't use that language!* to feel like her hand had just been invisibly smacked. How odd that a thirteen-year-old could make her feel ashamed, but maybe that was the root of it all. Abby was barely more than a child; could Elektra really murder someone so young and not hate herself every time she looked in the mirror . . . for the rest of her life?

Finally the ferry reached the mainland and docked, and then the three of them were in Mark's truck and on their way to the address Elektra had pried out of her agent over the cell phone. The placed turned out to be a grungy little pool hall tucked away in what was actually a pretty nice neighborhood, a hole in the wall where the people who weren't welcome anywhere else could gather, play pool, and drink beer a lot earlier in the day than was generally considered socially acceptable. When the three of them stepped through the door and Mark saw what they were coming into, he dropped behind Abby, effectively sandwiching the teenager between himself and Elektra. He followed Elektra's gaze and saw her zero in on two men at a pool table across the small room. One was a youngish guy with dirty hair drawn back in a pony tail; he was wearing a blue work shirt with his name—Jack—sewn above one pocket. He sighted in the shot, but missed.

"You're up, old man," Jack said. He stepped to the side as an older man with white hair and black sunglasses emerged from the shadows. He trailed his hand along the edge of the table, then stopped and held up his pool cue. "Two in the corner," he said. "Three off the rail, four in the far side."

Jack snorted and shook his head, grinning at a couple of his friends where they lounged against the wall. "You don't have to call all your shots, pops. Just the first one."

"That *is* the first one," the white-haired man said blandly. Without even lining up his shot, the older man reached over and hit the cue ball. Jack's jaw opened as the balls scattered and dropped into the pockets, just as his opponent predicted.

For no apparent reason, the white-haired man stopped and tilted his head, then turned and looked at the door where Mark, Abby, and Elektra had paused.

Jack licked his lips. "Uh . . . still your shot."

His coplayer nodded. "Nine and fourteen here and here," he pointed to the two end corners. "And eight in the side." An impossible-looking soft tap of his stick against the cue ball, and the balls sunk in just where he'd said they would. "Leave your money on the table," he said absently. He folded up his pool stick and headed for where the trio stood.

Elektra watched Stick approach and, incredibly, felt herself tremble. It had been years since she'd last seen him, that day when he'd thrown her out of the training camp. She had gone from potential Chaste to assassin—could she face him, after his rejection and after all the things she'd done in between? But why shouldn't she? After all, she was as much a child of his own making as she was of her temperament.

Mark glanced at her, and something on her face must have given her away. His eyes widened and he stared back at Stick. "*This* is the guy?" he asked incredulously. "He's *blind?*"

Elektra nodded, and while he didn't understand, Mark tapped Abby on the shoulder anyway. "Look," he said, digging a handful of coins out of his pocket. "Here's a dollar, Abs. Go play a few games of pinball."

Abby scowled, but she still took the money. "Why do I always have to miss the good stuff?"

A corner of Mark's mouth lifted. "When you get old enough to be there, you'll wish you *could* miss it."

Abby tossed her blond hair. "Does that mean life always sucks?"

This time he grinned outright. "Exactly." This time, Abby smiled too, then she headed for the machines in the corner. Mark watched her go, and when he turned back, Elektra was face-to-face with the blind guy she'd called Stick.

"Elektra Natchios," the blind man said calmly. "Same perfume. Same walk."

Elektra grimaced and rubbed her forearm with one hand, betraying her self-consciousness. "Listen," she began. "I'm not here for—"

"Same chip on the shoulder," Stick noted.

"Look," Elektra said in a low voice. She sounded very close to outright pleading with him. "Don't start, okay? This is Mark Miller. He needs your help."

"I've heard of him," Stick said flatly.

Mark looked startled. "How do you know who I—"

Stick's gesture toward another part of the pool hall, where it was darker and there were booths that would give them a little more privacy, stopped his question. "Over there."

Stick moved off, and Elektra and Mark followed. When they were settled, Stick said, "Tell us who you are, Mr. Miller."

Elektra sent Stick a frustrated look that even Mark could interpret—whoever this man was, he was way ahead of her and she was *not* happy about it. Mark had the distinct impression that kind of thing had happened before. After casting a glance toward his daughter to make sure she was all right—she was killing the pinball machines and a couple of the pool hall's regulars had gathered around to watch—Mark had the good grace to look a little ashamed as he finally owned up to his, and Abby's, history.

"I owned a bunch of gyms," he finally told her. "Martial arts schools." He glanced at her furtively, and she frowned and nodded, acknowledging his unspoken admission to lying to her earlier. "I wasn't a practitioner, just in the business part. And I took on a partner, for capital." He paused and picked at a spot on the battered wooden table. It was clear that he wished he didn't have to keep going.

Obligingly, Stick picked up where Mark had stopped. "Then Mr. Miller found out he was in business with the *Hand*." His sightless eyes still bored into Elektra, making her squirm despite her resolve to appear unconcerned. "You remember the Hand, Elektra?"

"They wanted something I couldn't give them," Mark put in. His fingers were still digging at the tabletop. "When I tried to walk away, they came after me."

This time he glanced at Stick, making Elektra frown. He wasn't telling her everything and Stick knew it. She didn't like being the only one in the dark. "And?" Stick prompted.

Mark hesitated. "They killed my wife, Abby's mom.

There was no drunk driver. We've been on the run ever since."

Elektra sat back and digested this. More lies—why would they go to such lengths, especially if Mark and his daughter had already removed themselves from the picture? There was something she was missing here, something that in the strain of being in Stick's company, she'd overlooked. Damn it, what was it? Never mind. If Mark Miller wouldn't come clean with her, he and his daughter were too dangerous to play with.

She leaned toward Stick. "The Hand is your business, not mine. *You* help them." Then she stood and sent a withering look down at Mark. "You're on your own."

A corner of Stick's mouth curled before she could walk away. "And yet you saved their lives and brought them here. Why? Some kind of penance? A down payment on your sins?" He let his mouth stretch into a full, knowing smile. "Ninjas have always been your specialty."

Elektra shrugged carelessly. "They're overrated," she said levelly, but her eyes said otherwise. "But what comes next will be worse." Despite her dire statement, she turned to stalk off, then realized Abby had abandoned her pinball machine and all the free games, leaving the booty for the other guys to play out. Before she could get any further, she heard Stick ask Mark, "Has Elektra told you what she does for a living?"

"She saved my life," Mark interrupted. "And my daughter's."

164

But Stick only smirked. "You landed on the lucky side of the street," he said pointedly. "Because most people, she—"

This time, Elektra lunged for Stick's throat. "Damn you, you son of a—"

And she barely had time to think about what a stupid idea *that* was.

Elektra didn't see him move, nor likely did anyone else. In no more than the blink of an eye, she went butt over head and then she was bent over the nearest pool table with his pool stick—the one that she'd sworn he'd had neatly folded up—thoroughly pinning her to the dirty felt surface. She made a sort of growl in her throat and realized that the room had already cleared out—no one in here wanted a piece of this fight.

"I guess blind guys are your weakness," Stick said mildly. He actually looked sorry. "Oh, Elektra—I had hoped you changed."

Beyond furious now, Elektra slapped the tip of the pool cue to the side and jumped to her feet. With a last, murderous glare at Stick, she spun and stalked out the door.

Mystified, Mark grabbed Abby by the elbow and went after her, while behind them Stick headed back toward the pool tables to drum up another game when the bar's customers came back inside.

Three feet from it, he stopped and looked up at nothing at all.

Someone, or some*thing*, had joined the game.

12

ELEKTRA WAS WAITING WHEN MARK AND ABBY came out of the bar. She was pacing back and forth in the alley like an enraged leopard, and they watched her without saying anything, not sure of the next step. "What do we do now?" Abby finally asked. She looked from her father to Elektra, then back again, but Mark didn't have an answer.

Elektra started to say something, then she noticed something on the graffiti-covered wall. She jerked to a stop and went over to the spray-painted image, peering at the brightly colored bricks. It looked like a bird, an ornate, stylized hawk that could've been a biker's tattoo. After a few moments her eyes widened and she backed away from the wall.

"You have to run," she finally said. Her gaze kept jumping back to the wall suspiciously. "As far as you can, as fast as you can. South America, Africa—change your name, change your appearance." She brushed the hair out of her face and regarded the two of them steadily. "Change *everything*."

Mark only looked at her as the real meaning behind

her words sank in, but Abby wasn't so tactful. "You're not coming with us."

Elektra blinked, then looked away. "No. I . . . can't."

"Why not?" Abby took a step toward Elektra, stepping in between Elektra and the wall so the older woman would have to look her in the eye. "Isn't that part of your code or something?"

Elektra rubbed her forehead tiredly. "I don't have a code, Abby. Stick has a code—even Kirigi has a code. But—"

Mark blinked at her. "Kirigi?"

Elektra waved him away. "Never mind."

Abby put her hands on her hips. "How are we going to defend ourselves?" she demanded.

Her father sighed and put a hand on her shoulder and pulled her back. "Abby, we'll be okay," he began.

But his daughter jerked out of his grasp. "No, Dad— we won't!" The teenager was practically stomping her foot to make him comprehend her words. "Wake *up*, Dad—we *won't!*"

Elektra's mouth worked. God, she didn't know *what* to do here—if she let Mark and Abby go, it meant certain death for both of them, but what else could she do? This wasn't her fight, and the odds against them were probably insurmountable. She wasn't—

The beady black eyes of the hawk painted on the wall behind Abby shifted suddenly, moving to the right and locking with Elektra's narrowed gaze. Incredibly, the finely detailed feathers along its wings started to bristle.

"Get in the car," Elektra whispered urgently. *"Now!"*

In a burst of abrupt color, the bird's painted image suddenly went 3-D, pulling free of the cracked surface of the wall and taking full shape. It flapped its wings frantically for a second or two to fluff out its feathers, then exploded free and rocketed down the alley. It banked right, then soared high into the air and disappeared over the rooftop.

Tattoo jerked and opened his eyes as his hawk tattoo slammed back into his upper arm with enough force to jerk him backwards. The bird melted into his skin, sliding along the flesh until it fit precisely into its rightful place. He blinked for a moment to clear his head of the avian's thoughts, then gave an evil grin.

"Tattoo," Kirigi said impatiently, "where are they?"

He rubbed his arm absently, then pointed past Kirigi. "Down the street and three blocks over, in the parking lot. With that assassin."

Kirigi's returning grin was quite a bit blacker. "We need to kill her first."

Tattoo looked up. "Should we do it now?"

Looking over from her spot at the edge of the roof where the five of them had gathered, Typhoid sent Kirigi a small, sleepy smile. "I can handle that."

Kirigi started to answer, then stopped and frowned

slightly. He turned back in the direction Tattoo had indicated and concentrated, trying to confirm with his mind what his senses were feeling. Yes—it was true. Of all people, Stick was down there, and he wasn't alone. Always one to show up when it was most inconvenient, the elder was accompanied by members of his precious Chaste. Kirigi knew Typhoid was waiting, but he took his time deciding, weighing his options. "No," Kirigi finally decided. "Not here." He inclined his head toward Tattoo. "Keep track of them."

Tattoo nodded, and his fingers reached up and began to once again stroke the hawk inked onto his upper arm.

They were in the pickup truck again, which frustrated Elektra no end. Elektra was driving this time, zipping down the interstate at a speed limit–defying eighty-five miles an hour, but it wasn't like that was going to do them any good. As far as she was concerned, they might as well paint a big bull's-eye on the hood, or maybe the roof, where the Hand's aim would be more accurate and put them all out of this ridiculous misery that much faster.

Mark was in the passenger seat, staying quiet and staring out the window. Maybe he was contemplating his coming death, maybe he was thinking about the possibility, no, *probability*, that his daughter was going to die right along with him and Elektra. Why didn't people think things through before they put themselves and their loved ones in these kinds of doomed situations? Elektra had suffered so much loss in her life that she had learned well the pain of having family members become collateral damage.

This time, anticipating a long drive, Abby had opted for the back seat of the oversized truck. Now she leaned forward, straining against her seatbelt and holding on to the back of the front seat, so she could talk to Elektra. "So you really kill people for a living?"

That was the thing about children. They didn't pull punches or monkey around with tact. Keeping her eyes on the road, Elektra nodded.

Abby paused, then asked simply, "Why?"

Elektra opened her mouth to answer, but suddenly all her thoughts were tumbling around in her head. Why, indeed? She was, she thought, still full of the anger that had never gone away after her mother's death—in fact, losing her father, then what she'd had, no matter how short and sweet, with Matt Murdock had only refilled the fury tank. Finally she said the only thing she could come up with. "It's what I'm good at."

Amazingly, this seemed to appease Abby, whose only response after a moment was, "Weird."

The teenager sat back then, apparently to brood over Elektra's words. Elektra drove on, occasionally glancing in the mirror to check on Abby and worrying about what she was thinking. Just the simple act of monitoring the girl nettled her—what was she doing here, anyway, driving down this highway and trying to save what was left of this average American family? It was ridiculous, and it wasn't like she'd ever have a chance to be a part of the Miller family, a *real* part of it. No matter how much she was attracted to Mark—and yes, faced with the coming disaster she thought she might as well be honest enough to admit that much— she was never going to be normal, she was never going to slide into the spot vacated by the dead Mrs. Miller. She didn't even *want* to.

Did she?

Of course not. She was Elektra, the Assassin. Men did not want lovers who killed for a living, and teenaged girls did not need assassins for role models.

The minutes stretched out, turning into several hours before Elektra turned off to get to the farm that had been her goal the entire time. Even this far away from any dense population or greenery, the driveway was long and lined with palm trees and a myriad of flowering plants. Farther off the little side road, she could see pine trees and bougainvillea bushes that had scattered scarlet December flowers blooming on them. When she finally got to the house, a rambling structure that probably had fourteen or fifteen rooms in it and was off the main road by a good three or four miles, Mc-Cabe was waiting on the front lawn, a Winchester twelve-gauge cradled comfortably in the crook of one

171

arm. As she brought Mark's truck to a stop, Elektra could hear the energetic popping of his gum through the open driver's side window.

He gave her a wry grin, but it didn't look very genuine. There were shadows beneath his eyes and he was being just a little too casual about her visit. "Well, well," he said cheerfully. "The reluctant assassin."

Elektra got out of the truck slowly, looking back at Abby. She'd fallen asleep sometime ago, and now the sounds of conversation and lack of motion were pulling her back into the here and now. "Sorry to drag you into this, McCabe."

The last traces of his grin disappeared and he only looked back at her. "Me, too," he said, and rubbed the back of his other hand nervously across his mouth.

Abby unbuckled her seat belt, then climbed groggily out of the back seat of the truck. When her gaze focused on McCabe, her eyes brightened with interest. "Hi," she said. Elektra's eyebrows rose and she fought a grin as Abby went into flirt mode. "I'm Abby. Who are you?"

McCabe's smile reluctantly returned, this time a little more on the genuine side. "And I'm wondering why *you're* here," he came back instead of answering. When Abby gave him a winsome grin, he looked like he was surrendering. He turned to face Mark, who'd gotten out of the truck and was eyeing McCabe suspiciously. He didn't offer to shake hands, and neither did Mc-

Cabe. "Plenty of bedrooms in the house," McCabe told him. "Help yourself to whatever you need."

Mark relaxed a bit. "Thank you." He glanced at Elektra, who motioned for him and Abby to go on without her. When they'd finally disappeared inside, she took a deep breath and readied herself to face the music. It wasn't long in coming.

"What are you doing?" McCabe asked. His voice was a lot sharper than the tone he'd used with Abby and Mark. When all Elektra would do was stare at the ground, he continued. "You're crashing on me, baby. I said you'd crash, and you're crashing."

She opened and closed her hands, feeling helpless. Her voice, when she answered, sounded small and uncertain. "I just want to get them someplace safe. Give them a chance."

McCabe didn't say anything for a long moment, then he exhaled and reached out one hand so he could squeeze her elbow. "They've got no chance, E." His voice held more emotion than she'd ever heard before and she could tell he was grinding his teeth as he talked. "They're already dead. Don't go down with them."

McCabe was right, of course—she knew that. She'd known it long before they'd arrived here. But she'd never been one to give up, or even necessarily listen to reason. "I need passports," she said by way of answering. "Plane tickets."

McCabe let go of her elbow and made a tiny sound of exasperation. When he spoke again, there was no trace of the feeling she'd heard before. "You pay for them," he said flatly. "Not me."

She nodded, feeling as though she'd just been terribly chastised by the gentlest teacher. She moved around him and went toward the house, and McCabe was still looking past her as if she wasn't even there. Things were awkward enough without her trying to engage in idle conversation, so Elektra left him alone with his thoughts and his weapon.

Gripping the shotgun's stock, with eyes that were just as piercing, McCabe was watching the hawk that watched him from the branches of a pine tree. . . .

13

ELEKTRA HAD HER SAIS OUT IN McCABE'S BASE-ment workshop and was carefully sharpening them with a whetstone when she heard someone call her name. She looked up automatically and her breath caught in her throat as she saw a younger version of herself descending the basement stairs—

No, that wasn't right.

She had to literally shake her head to clear it, and when she looked up again, she realized it was Abby. The teenager had changed her hair, dyed the blond color to a shade that exactly matched Elektra's. Even though Elektra realized now what the illusion had been, she still couldn't say anything or hide the stunned look on her face.

"What's the matter?" Abby asked when she caught Elektra's expression. "They told me I had to change my appearance, so I—"

"No," Elektra said quickly. "It looks . . . you look great." Elektra hoped she sounded sincere. Abby *did* look excellent, but it was still a shock when she realized how much the girl resembled her.

She could tell that Abby was pleased by the blush that crept across her cheeks, but in true teenager form, all the girl did was shrug carelessly. "Thanks." She pointed at the sais on McCabe's long workbench. "Can you show me how to use these things? The salad tongs?"

"Sais," Elektra corrected automatically.

"Sais," Abby repeated, then waited expectantly.

"And no, they're not for you." Elektra bent her head back to her work.

Abby crossed her arms, her expression melding to stubbornness. "I want to learn how to defend myself."

Elektra shook her head. "They're offensive weapons, meant for killing."

"You use them."

Elektra looked at the girl from beneath lowered lids. "I don't want you to be like me."

"I do," Abby said with rough honesty.

Elektra tried to think of something to say, but it was unnerving to argue with Abby now, almost as if she were arguing with her younger self. "You want to learn something?" Elektra finally asked. "Something really hard?"

Abby brightened. "Yeah. What?"

Elektra pointed to a chair off to the side. "Sit down."

Abby obeyed, her face bright with enthusiasm as Elektra pulled a chair around and sat directly in front of her.

"Now close your eyes."

The girl did, then reopened them immediately. "Oh, what is this—yoga?"

"No," Elektra told her. "It's kimagure. It can allow you to see what's going to happen before it happens." She paused, but she wasn't sure she could make Abby understand just how important learning this could be. "It's a lot more valuable than knowing how to use a weapon," she added.

Abby's eyes widened. "That's intense. How do you do it?"

Elektra struggled to maintain her concentration. "You concentrate—meditate. Learn to see everything around you. It's not easy."

"How long did it take you to master?"

Elektra inhaled. "Well, I never really completed my training. I only knew enough to keep myself alive. But true masters—like Stick—have learned to use their kimagure in many ways." She opened her eyes just enough to peer at Abby. "They can bring the dead back." Abby looked unconvinced and Elektra sighed inwardly. It would take time. "Just breathe," she told the girl.

"I'm breathing," Abby said. "I'm *always* breathing."

"And shut up."

Abby finally tried to do what Elektra had said, but the effort lasted only a few moments. She couldn't resist a peek, just to see if Elektra really *was* doing what she said—yep. She closed her eyes again and tried to count her breathing, but she was too prone to getting restless. This wasn't like the unconscious counting she did—breathing was something she always did. In another second or two, she started fidgeting.

"Just sit quietly," Elektra said with her eyes still closed.

Abby tried again, to no avail. After a few moments, it seemed like her legs started swinging of their own account, one foot bouncing up and down. Elektra, of course, somehow knew she was doing all this, even though she'd never opened her eyes; she reached out with one hand and touched Abby's knee. That stilled her legs, but then Abby made a big production out of trying to breathe in the way she *thought* she should, inhaling and exhaling in exaggerated form.

"Shhhhhh," Elektra whispered.

Well, Abby thought as her expression went sour, this is just *boring*. She sat there, staring at Elektra, until she couldn't stand it anymore and finally leaned in as close to Elektra as she dared without actually touching her. Did the woman even know she was there? She was so still and her breathing was so shallow and even that she could have been sleeping while sitting upright. Besides, what was the big deal about this, anyway? She wanted to learn how to fight, and this didn't have anything to do with *that*.

Tilting her head and studying Elektra—who was really pretty—Abby grinned to herself, then exhaled very quietly, directly into Elektra's face.

No response.

She sat back, but still made an effort to stay quiet. There was a piece of thread hanging from the hem of her T-shirt, and Abby picked at it stealthily, finally working it free. It ended up being about two inches long, which was just the right length to really pester someone. Taking the thread between her thumb and forefinger, Abby reached forward and just barely touched it to the front of Elektra's neck, then moved it enough so that it should have tickled.

Nothing, which was pretty impressive when Abby considered that she herself would have cracked up almost right from the start. Still, she was bored and this wasn't a bit of fun. What exactly was she supposed to be learning, anyway? She twisted on her chair and looked around, hoping to find something else that would distract her.

Elektra suddenly grabbed her around the waist with both hands.

Abby shrieked and came off the chair, and then they were both laughing and giving up on the lesson. They were still laughing when Mark and McCabe walked into the room.

Mark looked from one to the other. "What's so funny?"

"Yoga!" Abby was giggling and gasping for air. "Yoga's hilarious!" Now Elektra started laughing again.

Mark had no idea what his daughter was talking about, but that was fine—at least she was having fun for a change.

Before he could question them further, McCabe broke in. "Hey, guys." He dropped a pile of papers and things on the table. "Passports, plane tickets, contacts."

Abby leaned forward eagerly, pawing through the small green books until she found her own passport and opened it. Her nose wrinkled up as she read the text surrounding the photograph. "Oh, give me a break! 'Evelyn'? I'm not going to be a fri—an *Evelyn*—"

"Get used to it, babe," McCabe interrupted. "It's your new name." His gaze was bland, as if he were purposely distancing himself from all of them. "Get some sleep," he said crisply. "You leave at dawn."

Night came to McCabe's farm at the end of another one of those spectacular sunsets. This time, instead of the pink- and red-painted clouds hovering over a shimmering twilight ocean, the clouds capped snow-covered mountains in the distance and bled red onto the hillsides in between. Rather than looking beautiful, Mark thought the whole thing looked vaguely ominous, like something that should precede the end of the world. It didn't give him a warm and fuzzy feeling.

He sat on the side of Abby's bed after tucking her in,

trying not to think about the earlier sunset while his daughter wanted to talk about things he'd rather avoid altogether. Maybe, as she'd suggested earlier, he ought to "wake up." Were they even going to make it through this? He had to believe they would—he didn't have any other choice. If he didn't have hope enough for the both of them, then they had nothing; her mother was gone and now it was his job to be the sole leader and the protector of his child. He would blame himself for the death of his wife for the rest of eternity, but he would *not* let the Hand take his daughter.

Abby's voice broke into his thoughts. "I hate lying," she said. She was irritable at having to sleep in her street clothes—something Elektra had insisted on in case they had to leave quickly—and she sounded peevish and tired. Of course she was—what they were enduring would wear down any normal adult, and his daughter was barely into her teens. "Why can't we tell her?" Abby demanded.

Mark shook his head sharply. "She's a *killer*, Abs. She—"

But it was clear Abby was having none of that. "Dad, she *saved* us!"

"Because she doesn't know who we are," Mark explained patiently. Sometimes he felt like an old VCR tape stuck in a defective machine, rewinding and playing the same scene over and over. "If she knew, she would—"

Now Abby's face pinched a little, her nose going red as she fought not to cry. "She's my *friend*," she insisted.

"Your friend?" Mark stared at her and felt his patience start to slip a notch. An internal voice reminded him that she was barely more than a child and prone to trusting easily. "You don't know anything about her!"

Abby's voice rose. "She's the only one I have left! I don't want to die without—"

Now Mark's voice, shaking with anger, drowned out his daughter's. "Abby, you are *not* going to die! Don't say that—*ever!* Or I'll—" He snapped his mouth shut to choke off his own words, then leaned over and kissed her on the forehead instead. She didn't push it, but he could see the disbelief on her face, and it was killing him. If Abby didn't believe he could protect her, that she actually had a future beyond today or tomorrow, then how could he believe in himself?

Elektra heard Mark coming long before she saw him, of course. Even though he was making an effort to walk quietly, his footsteps rang clearly in her hearing as though they were coming from a three-hundred-pound ape. He sat heavily on the lawn chair a few feet away, then stared at the floor of the porch, poking at the boards half-absently, half-angrily with the toe of his shoe. His face was tight and angry, and Elektra didn't have to ask why—she hadn't heard the words between him and Abby, but the volume and the tone had reached her through the window.

"How is she?" Elektra finally asked, being careful to keep her voice down.

Mark shrugged, then ducked his head and nodded to himself. "Still alive . . . thanks to you."

But Elektra shook her head. "Don't thank me, Mark. You don't really know what I was—"

"What you were doing there?" Mark finished for her. "Sure I do. You were there to kill us." He looked at her wearily. "We suspected it from the minute you moved into the Wheelwright place."

Elektra sat back and considered this. She hadn't thought about it until now, but if she put all the pieces together and then inserted Mark and Abby's behavior, they'd certainly come close to that complete picture, wouldn't they? It all fit—the constant vigilance, the paranoia, the evasive answers to her questions. It was kind of ironic that they'd known who she'd come there for before she had . . . and they'd been her target.

"Ever since her mother was killed," Mark said in a low voice, "we've been looking over our shoulders." He rubbed the knuckles of both hands. "I brought this whole mess on us. I didn't pull the trigger, but I loaded the gun. I put it in their hands."

"Mark," Elektra said, "come on—"

He held up his hand. "I brought this on Abby. If I hadn't gone after that money, trying to be a big shot—"

Elektra found herself reaching out and resting her hand on his arm. "Don't," she said. "It's easy to cut your heart open, but it won't help."

Mark looked up at her in surprise, then their gazes met and locked. It wasn't the first time she'd been caught by Mark's attractiveness, but it *was* the most powerful; that he was enamored of her just gave everything a double dose of desire.

Elektra saw it coming, and tried to stop it. "I'm probably not a good person to . . ." She hesitated, not finding the right words. "Especially now. I have nothing to give—"

"I'm not asking for anything," he said, and then she wasn't sure how it happened, but suddenly they went from her hand stroking his arm to being in each other's arms, kissing and holding on to each other as if nothing and no one else existed in the universe. His hands felt so good on her back, his lips fit hers almost perfectly, warm and soft, and when his mouth moved to her throat all she wanted to do was throw her head back and—

It took every bit of willpower she had to pull away. "I'm sorry," he said breathlessly. He looked from her shoulders to his hands as if he couldn't figure out how she'd ended up in his arms . . . or maybe why she wasn't still there.

Elektra's heart was pounding as hard in her chest as if she'd just had a rip-roaring good fight with someone.

"Oh, I really hated that," she managed. She inclined her head toward the window, a silent reminder that Abby was just on the other side of a pane of glass.

The expression on Mark's face said he knew she was right, but he didn't like it. She couldn't help that, and just to keep things temptation-free, she got up and hurried inside, leaving Mark to find his way back into Abby's room and sleep, fully clothed, on a comforter pallet on the floor at the side of Abby's bed.

Elektra slept fitfully, twisting and turning and floating in and out of awareness, her nerves working on her and refusing to let her drop completely into slumber. The night had cooled considerably and now a chill wind was blowing into McCabe's ranch house through any number of windows left open, including the one in Elektra's room. This time when the air hit her, her eyelids snapped open and she was suddenly awake, logic and reason fully functional, reflexes on high alert.

McCabe was standing at the foot of her bed, holding his shotgun.

Elektra rolled and jammed her hands up and under her pillows; they came back out armed with a sai in each one. As she spun and readied them, McCabe raised his shotgun, and if she didn't know any better, she would have sworn he was aiming straight at her—

He fired at something on the windowsill.

The gun's report was a huge thing in the darkness,

shaking the walls and reverberating around the house. The flash was bright and painful, enough to make her eyes water, as something, a shape that was blacker than the darkness outside the window, screeched and disappeared. As Elektra squinted to readjust her eyesight and stared at the two or three black feathers fluttering to the floor, it wasn't hard to guess what had been spying on her in her sleep. She closed her eyes in a quick moment of concentration and—

—*she could see them, Kirigi and his crew of ne'er-do-well murderers, approaching the house from all directions.*

She blinked away the kimagure image just as Mark and Abby stumbled into her room, their faces shocked into wakefulness by the noise of the gun blast. Elektra was already on her feet and yanking on her jacket. "They're here," she said flatly.

Mark grabbed Abby by the elbow and motioned at Elektra. "Come on—let's get to the truck."

Elektra only looked at him. "We won't make it."

Mark swallowed. "But—"

"Trust me," Elektra told him. "It's too late."

"Use the cellar," McCabe said. He was still standing at the end of the bed and staring out the window, but there was a ratcheting sound as he primed the shotgun again. "There's a tunnel that'll take you out past the orchard to the woods. Head north."

Elektra's eyes widened. She'd had no idea. "What about you?" she demanded.

He shrugged and gave her a lopsided grin, and she could hardly believe it. This was the man who'd thought she was a fool for not just doing her job and killing Mark and Abby—the same man who was now putting his life on the line to help her save the two people she should have eliminated days ago. He would pay for this, and pay dearly, and they both knew it. She couldn't do anything but hug him fiercely, and she saw him close his eyes for just a moment. Just that pause, that tiny thing, made her wonder if she had missed something in her relationship with McCabe all these years. It was a heartbreaking thought that now it would be forever too late to find out.

"Elektra, come *on!*" Abby cried, and McCabe pushed her away, propelling her toward the door to the cellar. He didn't say anything else as he turned and strode in the other direction, gun now held tight and ready. The last time Elektra saw McCabe, he was headed out the back door to meet Kirigi and his fighters in the dawn.

He was going to die over this, and he knew it.

There were very few things that McCabe regretted in his life, but never revealing his feelings for Elektra Natchios was the biggest of those. There were a whole lot of reasons he hadn't, of course—never mix business with pleasure, rejection, the potential for a volatile and ultimately failed relationship with such a dangerous woman. He wished he had that kimagure thing that Elektra had; he would have used it to see what would have happened if he'd just turned around and kissed her on any one of a dozen different occasions. But he didn't have it, and now he would never know the answer anyway.

McCabe could see one of Kirigi's men heading toward the house at full speed, and he brought the shotgun up, aimed and fired, then fired again, and again. He was generally a damned fine shot, but this guy was remarkably agile, and as he came up fast on McCabe's position, he recognized him as Kinkou, one of Kirigi's younger punks. He made dodging McCabe's target practice seem easy as he ran from a tree to McCabe's car—where, incredibly, he momentarily balanced on the tip of the *antenna*—to the shed, all without losing his balance or tripping on a single stone. He was so impossible to hit that he might as well have been surrounded by an invisible force field.

McCabe fired until he felt he was no longer safe, then he backed up until the door shielded him, reloaded, and kept trying.

There simply wasn't anything else he could do.

Elektra could hear the sounds of McCabe's shotgun blasts, each one getting more and more muffled as she and the other two went farther into the cellar. It took only a few seconds to find the door, then they were through it and pulling it shut behind them, fastening it with a slide bar they found on the other side. Now, as they raced through an underground passageway barely lit by the faint glow of low-usage battery lights, the blasts went to faint thuds and finally disappeared altogether. She didn't want to think about what that meant for the man who had been her business partner—and unacknowledged friend—for the past several years.

It didn't take long until they came to the end of the tunnel, where they found a small metal ladder leading upward to a trap door. Mark would have led the way, but Elektra forced him behind her and climbed out first, blinking at the sudden light after the tunnel's darkness. When she was sure it was safe, she motioned for Mark and Abby to follow, and by the time they emerged from the hole in the ground she had her bearings and was leading them as fast and far away from McCabe's as she could.

McCabe was doing all right—at least that's what *he* thought—until someone surprised him from behind; the guy must have snuck in from the other side of the house using the shotgun blasts—loud enough to make McCabe's ears ring—as cover. McCabe whirled and fired automatically, point-blank into the chest of a man bigger than anyone he'd ever seen in his life. Then McCabe's mouth fell open in amazement as he watched his buckshot literally *flatten* against the broad, chocolate-colored chest. He back-stepped quickly and slammed the door, but that was as useless as drawing a curtain—in two seconds, the huge man had smashed the door into nothing but toothpicks.

McCabe knew all the players, he always had. When Typhoid, Tattoo, Kinkou, and finally Kirigi himself strolled through the doorway, he wasn't foolish enough to think that there was anything on the face of this earth that was going to save him.

But he'd be *damned* if he'd show them any fear.

"Circus in town?" He sounded a lot more mocking than he felt—he really hadn't planned on dying this young. "Where are the midgets?" When no one laughed, he sighed. "You might as well kill me now, 'cause I'm not talking."

Kirigi's smile was full of darkness. "Talking's not necessary," he said. "But I accept the first part of your proposal." Before McCabe could respond, Kirigi grabbed the man's head in both of his hands and lifted his upper body off the floor.

McCabe suddenly felt like his head was going to explode. Kirigi's hands pressed into his scalp, going through the hair and skin and bone and right into his brain . . . or maybe it just felt like it, then the leader of the band of killers going after Elektra began talking.

"They're in the woods," Kirigi said softly. "Kinkou, Stone, Typhoid—" He pointed north. "That way. *Hurry.*"

The others rushed to obey Kirigi, and then it was just McCabe and him, staring into each other's eyes. Kirigi released him with a shove and McCabe fell hard to the floor, biting back the shout of pain as his head thumped hard against the kitchen's ceramic tile. Then he couldn't do anything but lie there—couldn't move, or think of a way out. There was no escape.

But he could still talk. He still had something to say. Oh, yes.

"Hey, dickhead," McCabe ground out. His voice sounded thick and wet, but that was okay. He was still going to get his point across. "I'll bet you a thousand bucks you're dead before Elektra is."

McCabe saw Kirigi's sword leave its sheath and swing toward his neck, heard the other man's final words to him before he even registered what was going to happen.

"*Shut up.*"

14

ELEKTRA HAD NEVER THOUGHT A FOREST COULD seem so ominous.

This one was, though—like something out of a nightmare version of *Snow White*, except in this telling of the classic fairy tale the seven dwarfs were compacted into Kirigi and his killers and she and her helpers were doomed. It was sunrise and bright, yet every bush seemed alive and filled with dark movement, nothing more than a place for something evil to hide, some assassin or hideous tattoo come to life. The previous night's storm had left its mark here, too: the forest floor was thick with wet, sticky leaves, and while that damp carpet should have quieted their footsteps and helped them along, she knew it would also help those who were chasing them. She knew there would soon be other things helping in the hunt, too, ugly bits and pieces of Tattoo's animal menagerie given animation and sent to track them for their master.

They were deep into the woods when Elektra led them into a thick stand of trees, and for a moment—a very *short* moment—they were out of range of the pry-ing eyes. Abby was next and Mark hurried after her, his feet heavy on the muddy ground, pounding forward until he saw that Elektra had held up her hand for them to stop. They could all hear Kirigi's team coming— there was nothing at all stealthy about their pursuit— and Elektra gestured for Mark and Abby to crawl under a canopy of fallen trees, a sort of deadwood cover that might conceal them.

Abby balked and started to back up. "No," she protested. "I want to help—"

Her father ignored her, grabbing her by the wrist and yanking her with him beneath the branches. When they were fully hidden, a quick snap of Elektra's wrist sent a handful of throwing stars into the vine-covered trunk of a nearby tree and leading upward into the branches; she scampered up them as though they were stairs.

Then Elektra sat back to wait.

Such pretty flowers, Typhoid Mary thought. So fragrant and . . . *delicate*.

She trailed her fingers over the white blossoms that had been planted in the decorative pots on McCabe's front porch, then watched them wither and die at her touch, curling in on themselves until they were nothing more than tiny brown shells. Yes, that was better, *much* better.

"Typhoid . . ."

She jumped as Kirigi's voice startled her out of her reverie, then she looked up and smiled at him. He put his hands on her shoulders and turned her so that their gazes met, his clear and black, hers equally dark, but faraway and dreamy. His mind pried into hers, but she didn't care at all.

He grimaced suddenly and pushed her away. "What repulsive thoughts you have," he said. His normally calm face twisted, and she couldn't help but grin even as he steered her ahead of him and they followed the others on the hunt for Elektra and the treasure. Her touch would clear the way for them in the woods, withering the leaves and cracking the branches into nothing but twigs. Soon there would be nowhere for their prey to hide.

Despite his immense size, Stone was the first of Kirigi's crew to flounder upon their hiding place.

Elektra watched him from her safe perch above, feeling the tree vibrate with each step that took him closer to Mark and Abby's concealment. So far, so good—no one had moved and the two were doing well at being still. If they just stayed that way, Stone would blunder right by them and—

A branch crackled in the bushes.

Elektra silently ground her teeth. Abby, little Miss Can't-Be-Still, must have moved, and it was a terrible error—they'd almost been in the clear, but her fidgeting had given away her and her father's position.

It was too much of a stretch to hope that Stone hadn't heard it. For a moment, the huge man acted like that was exactly it, then he gave a wide-mouthed grin and looked directly at the spot in which father and daughter were secreted.

He might be looking forward, but he should have had eyes in the back of his head.

Elektra dropped to the ground right behind him, coming down so softly and without sound that she might have been a graceful cat landing on a bed of cotton. Stone hefted a club that looked more like a caveman's weapon than anything else and started to move forward; when he was in exactly the right position, Elektra expertly spun one of her sais until it was pointed in the correct direction, then stabbed him dead center in the back.

Clank!

Then she was holding up the sai and looking at the broken blade in disbelief.

Stone turned, his mouth stretched in a hideously self-satisfied grin. She'd heard stories of this man, of how his flesh was impenetrable, the skin as hard as the stone for which he was named, but she'd never really believed it. This was an awfully bad time to find out the legends were actually true.

195

Before she could decide what to do next, Stone's ham-sized hand wrapped around her upper arm, then he lifted her body and flung her away like she weighed no more than a child's rag doll. Usually she enjoyed the sensation of flying, but never like this, when she knew it was going to—

"*Uh!*"

—end in the particularly painful moment when her flesh slammed into something a whole lot harder. Worse than that—Elektra could take a little pain—was hearing Abby's cry of dismay when Elektra hit a tree about fifteen feet away. *That* was bad, because it turned Stone's attention away from her and sent it right back to where Mark and Abby were hiding. So much for concealment.

For a single, breathless moment, Elektra thought he was going to miss them. She was still picking herself up when he lumbered over to the deadfall where they were hiding and stopped, tilting his head as though he just wasn't quite sure if this was the right place. Then he took two steps past the pile of dead branches—

—whirled back, and started beating on it with his club.

Elektra hauled herself upright with a silent snarl as Mark and Abby gave up their hiding place under the massive assault, flushed out of it like terrified rabbits. They tried to back away, but Stone's last swung grazed Mark, just barely, on the side of the head; even so, his heavy weapon was enough to send the lighter man sprawling. Grinning madly, Stone advanced and raised his weapon.

THWACK!

Elektra cracked Stone hard on the back of the head with a branch as thick as her forearm.

"Huh?" He turned in a slow circle and regarded her with small, black eyes, like a dull-witted ape. He wasn't hurt—she hadn't expected he would be—but at least annoying him would give Abby time to get her father on his feet and run. She gestured at him with a lot more bravado than she felt. "Come on—let's see if you can give as good as you get."

As expected, Stone lumbered toward her. They circled each other warily—as stupid as he might seem, he knew better than to underestimate Elektra. She was faster—always—but in the end, he had invulnerability on his side; ultimately she ended up on the defensive, throwing punches and kicks that did nothing to affect him as she was forced to back away.

Finally, she had nowhere else to go.

Her back was against the trunk of a good-sized tree. She could have dodged around it, but what would be the point? Nothing she could do would hurt Stone, and he would just keep coming after her. One way or another, this had to end, and she'd seen Mark and Abby escape behind him.

With the familiar psychotic grin on his face, Stone

reached out for her and started to take a step forward, then looked down at his feet in confusion. No good—his heavy body had sunk into the soft earth and mud and he was firmly stuck. It didn't matter to him; rather than chase after her, he lifted his massive club, aimed it at her neck, and put all his weight into flinging it. The motion was so hard and powerful that the club went forward like a rocket-propelled battering ram.

But Elektra was gone before it got there, already hanging from a branch above him in the tree. The heavy club spun into the spot where she'd been and punched a huge hole right through the trunk. Overhead, Elektra swung her body around the branch like a gymnast, landing upright, then speeding down the backside of the tree's trunk, using her leg muscles to pound it downward toward Stone. He stared at her, not impressed.

"A tree?" he rumbled. "Rock beats paper."

He didn't bother to move as the trunk finally cracked and the tree tumbled toward him, then suddenly his face changed and he belatedly realized he was wrong about the game's rules and he needed to run. But it was too late for that—his weight had made him sink even farther into the mud, the moist ground closing around his huge, heavy feet like quicksand around a rotting log. He wasn't going *anywhere*, not now—

WHAM!

—not ever.

Elektra looked triumphantly down at him. "Nope. *Paper* beats rock."

Even invulnerability had tension points, and sometimes the best assassins know just how to hit them.

Kirigi heard the crash from the woods and knew instantly that it meant Stone's death. He shook his head in disgust. Stone had had his uses, but time and time again the universe had proved that brawn was no match for brains, and this was just another example. He headed in the direction of the noise with Tattoo and Typhoid following, then looked over at Tattoo. They'd come to a small clearing and Kirigi didn't have to say anything for Tattoo to know what was expected of him. Tattoo sank to the ground and sat cross-legged, then slipped out of his robe. His torso was naked underneath, dressed only in vibrant shades of ink. As the others fanned out, he flexed his muscles and closed his eyes, concentrating; an instant later the ink began to ripple across his skin. Soon the eyes of all the creatures inked on his body blinked, slowly at first as they awoke, then faster. The patterns shifted, then started to bleed off his body. Kirigi left Tattoo there to do his job, and before he and Typhoid had gone five feet, all the animals that had been emblazoned on Tattoo's skin had leapt free and were streaking past to disappear into the forest in glowing blurs of blue.

*　　*　　*

With the side of his head throbbing, Mark dragged himself upward, then pulled Abby to her feet. He'd wanted to run as Elektra had faced off with the guy who'd found them, but his daughter was having none of it. She didn't understand that his first priority was her rather than Elektra. She probably never would, and so he had resorted to the physical and just dragged her as fast as he could. "Abby?"

She gripped his hand. "I'm all right," she said, and brushed at her jeans.

"Come on," he said. "Elektra got him—let's get as much distance between them and us as we can—"

A bone-chilling growl froze them where they stood.

Mark's mouth opened and he tried to back up, tried to get his daughter away from the snarling tiger that was literally inches away from her face. The creature was real . . . but not—it was a strange, glowing blue, but he had no doubt it was just as dangerous as the normal striped species. Where had this beast come from? One step, then another, and something else rumbled from behind them; when Mark clutched at Abby and turned, they were directly in the path of a growling wolf.

The colors on the animals heightened suddenly, burning until they were iridescent and painfully bright. Desperate, Mark's hand found a thick branch; he hefted it threateningly, but the wolf still crept forward, its teeth drawn back over blood-red gums. Finally,

Mark swung the branch. The wolf's response was to lunge forward and snap its teeth closed hard enough to cleave all the way through the wood.

Fear for his daughter almost choked Mark. He leapt sideways, going for Abby, when something long and dark shot over his head—one of Kirigi's assassins. Before he could get to Abby, the flat of the man's blade sent him sprawling and the killer had Abby by the throat.

"Elektra!"

The assassin tightened his hold and choked off anything else Abby was going to call out, then grinned evilly at both of them.

With the beasts on one side, and this man holding Abby on the other—

They were trapped.

15

NOW THAT STONE WAS DEAD, ELEKTRA SPRINTED in the direction of Abby's voice. They had to be right up here—

"Assassin!"

She skidded to a stop at the sound of Kinkou's voice, then saw that he had Abby pinned in front of him. Before she could process everything that was going on, something passed between Mark and Abby, a look, a thought, *something*. Whatever it was, it calmed them both instantly, right in front of Elektra's eyes; Mark stopped his trembling and went utterly calm, seemed almost resigned. Elektra wouldn't understand why until later, but Mark glanced at his daughter and nodded.

"*Finally*," Abby said. She sounded strangely joyful.

Elektra saw Abby's hand drop away from where she had been trying to pry Kinkou's forearm away from her throat. It was such a small thing and it seemed to happen so slowly—nearly in slow motion—that Elektra almost didn't notice it: Abby's bracelet slipped off her wrist and fell into her hand, then the girl extended it like a chain. Elektra had known the bracelet was composed of warrior beads, so subconsciously she'd also always known it was long; it simply hadn't registered until now.

Until Abby whirled it once, switched it to her other hand, then snapped it up and out—

—and wrapped it around Kinkou's neck.

A single, well-timed and balanced yank whipped the killer over her right shoulder and landed him flat on his back on the ground for the first time in his life.

With the wind knocked out of him, Kinkou barely got the words out for his cohort. "Kirigi! The assassin—"

Elektra registered the arrival of Kirigi and Typhoid Mary, but she was still shocked at this radical change in Abby. She gaped at the girl as, in another fluid and practiced move, Abby pulled off her necklace. Then she dropped into a fighting stance with both necklace and bracelet whirling in her hands like deadly twin *kusari-fundos*—ninja fighting chains. Before Elektra could fully digest what was happening, Abby swung around and sent the end of one of the chains directly into the eye of the crouching, slavering wolf that was almost upon her.

The beast howled and dissolved, leaving nothing but blue haze as somewhere in the forest they heard a muffled cry of pain from Tattoo. With his creature injured, was he bleeding, the ink oozing from his skin like black blood? He must be, because now the rest of his animals were snapping out of existence, leaving nothing but a smoking blue glow as they returned to their master.

Kinkou had pulled himself up and he came forward again, but Elektra shoved him backward before he could strike. He did an admirably agile backflip away and landed on his feet right in front of Mark, and the only thing that kept Mark from being gutted was that he had already turned and was moving toward his daughter. Kinkou's sword left a six-inch slash across the back of Mark's shoulder; it hurt, but it wasn't deep enough to incapacitate him. Kinkou raised his blade again, then found himself in the middle of Abby's beads as she sped forward to protect her father. They spun and twisted and stung Kinkou in a hundred places before he could take a breath, but he went after her anyway—after all, they were mostly just wooden beads with a few copper ones tossed in for decoration, not the metal chains of a true fighting weapon. Then Elektra was there, and Abby's father, and all three of them were all tangled up.

Kirigi and Typhoid circled the struggling foursome, watching as Abby demonstrated the martial arts skills she had previously kept such a secret from Elektra. She was quite impressive for a youngster, and Kirigi couldn't help smiling as he enjoyed the entertainment.

"She *is* a little treasure, isn't she?" he asked, glancing over at Typhoid.

But Typhoid only shrugged and turned up her nose, perhaps out of jealousy. Kirigi smiled wider. "You wanted to kill the assassin," he said quietly. "Do it now."

Finally, something that pleased Typhoid Mary. She slid toward the fighters, moving carefully closer as Kirigi unsheathed his sword and joined her. They crouched at the edge of the fight with Kirigi waiting to join in, then Typhoid unobtrusively slid around to the rear of the nearest hedge. She scurried up a tree trunk until she was directly overhead. Kinkou leaped at Abby as Tattoo staggered into the edge of the clearing where they'd all faced off, but Abby's beads, a double length this time, easily pulled Kinkou off his feet; before she could relax her wrist and withdraw the bracelet in one hand, a spider, the last and least of Tattoo's little flesh companions, skittered up her arm.

Abby shrieked and jerked away as she slapped at it, trying to get it off her. She wasn't sure where it had gone, and she twisted one way, then another, momentarily distracted from the more imminent danger of Kinkou. When he caught her attention again, she completely missed the spider as it morphed colors and sunk into the fabric of her jacket sleeve—Kinkou was nearly upon her and she didn't have enough room to retaliate with either of her personal versions of the kusaris.

But no matter the turn of events, Elektra wasn't about to let anything happened to Abby—she'd been through far too much to quit now. She grabbed Kinkou's wrist before he could hit Abby, then sidestepped the palm strike he aimed at her cheekbone, coming in under his arm and ramming her shoulder up, hard, into his armpit. A little guidance downward on the back of his neck with her right forearm threw him off balance; she jammed her right knee up and into his groin, and that sent the killer face-forward into the dirt.

Mark saw the already wounded Tattoo go to his knees as Elektra reversed and caught him on the side of the head with a crescent kick, but there was no time to take Abby and run; amazingly, Kinkou came right back up, this time directing his full animosity toward Abby. Mark managed to lurch into his path and threw what he thought was a perfect punch; Kinkou easily dodged it. In fact, he tilted backward, flipping onto his head and gifting Mark with a nasty kick right in the face as he did it.

Mark dropped, gasping, but this was his daughter he was trying to protect. Abby was everything to him, and he, too, was up again, willing to die to keep her safe if he had to. He pulled himself to his knees, then was dismayed to see—knowing all the while that he had neither the speed nor the skill to get out of the way—Kinkou come at him with a perfect spinning kick. As Tattoo struggled upright yet again and Elektra stepped between him and Abby a few feet away, Mark could only lie on the ground and twist in pain.

Kinkou was delighted—at last he could be done with this *gaijin* and be about the more important business of finishing off the assassin. He would kill Mark Miller as Kirigi had finished off Elektra's agent: execution style, quick and bloody. To be sure he would have enough power in his blow, Kinkou lifted his knife as high over his head as he could—

Somewhere inside Mark was a little more strength, a little more willpower. He pulled on everything he had, and before Kinkou could swing downward, he propelled himself forward and rolled, taking the killer down like a human bowling ball. Kinkou tilted to one side and the surprise was enough to make him drop the knife he'd been about to plunge into Mark's chest. Kinkou's body went backward and, incredibly, finally stopped when it was just barely still above the ground—he looked as if he was *floating* only a few inches above it. He sent Mark a triumphant smile, but it blinked away as he saw Mark had picked up his knife.

Too late he realized that showing off had placed him in the worst position possible; when he tried to come back up, Mark jammed Kinkou's blade downward as hard as he could, slicing through flesh and bone and pinning Kinkou to the ground. He had time only to bellow in fear and pain; then his eyes went wide and blank and the familiar ugly green light began to spill from his body. Spent now, Mark crawled away just in time to avoid the rancid white flames that exploded from the dead man's flesh and burned him away to nothing.

Elektra was relieved—and a little amazed—to see Mark best Kinkou, but that's what could happen when a fighter underestimated his opponent. She and Abby were turning to face the coming Kirigi and she could also finally ask Abby the question that had burned into her mind the instant she'd seen the teenager twirling her bracelet and necklace so efficiently. "Who *are* you?"

Abby didn't answer. From her position a few feet away, she suddenly jerked her arm at something behind Elektra. "Elektra, *look OUT!*"

Elektra whirled—

And went right into the arms of Typhoid Mary.

The evil woman had swung down from the branch directly above Elektra and propelled herself body to body, right into her. Elektra went down with Typhoid on top of her, and before she could react, Typhoid planted her mouth on Elektra's and kissed her. Elektra went woozy instantly, trying ineffectively to push Typhoid away. It didn't even take Typhoid any effort to simply hold on.

Typhoid pushed up and onto her hands as she looked derisively at Elektra as her head lolled. "*This* is the legend? The one they talk about in whispers?" She sneered. "I am *not* impressed." Before Abby could think of what to do, Typhoid pulled Elektra's face forward and kissed her again, pumping unseen poison deep in her victim's body. Elektra twitched in her arms as the leaves beneath Typhoid's palms turned black and crumbled.

Abby gasped and Typhoid lifted her head, focusing on the girl. Ah—her *real* target! This one was done for anyway, so she abandoned Elektra and reached for Abby, stretching out her arms as her fingernails went black with anticipation—

But no. Kirigi's hand fell heavily on her shoulder, stopping her.

Abby, however, was far from finished. She jumped forward, placing herself in the space between Elektra and the other two, chains spinning smartly in the air.

But to face Kirigi, she was going to have to do better than that.

She whipped one of the jewelry chains toward his face, and he simply sidestepped the beads as if they weren't there, then reached a hand forward and grabbed the weapon, halting its progress without so much as a whimper. He gave her a dark smile and suddenly snapped it back at her; the copper and wood beads curled around Abby's neck and tightened, and then she was turning and being reeled toward him like a helpless fish on a line. "The war is over," he said gleefully, and reached for her.

A stick, old and well-worn, whistled through the air in front of them and neatly parted the length of chain between Kirigi and Abby's neck.

"The war's just begun," Stick said calmly as he stepped in front of Abby.

"Blind man!" Kirigi exclaimed as Abby stumbled backward and yanked the beads away. He looked disgusted.

Typhoid hissed in frustration, but seemed disinclined to attack. Satisfied that she wasn't a threat, Stick calmly turned to face the sound of Kirigi's voice. Abby started forward, but her father grabbed her and held her back, staring at the whitehaired man, the one they'd seen in the bar and whom Elektra had called Stick. Worse was Kirigi; with his sword unsheathed, he loomed over Elektra's spasming body. He seemed to terrify everyone who came in contact with him.

Except Stick.

Kirigi scowled and concentrated, trying to use kimagure on his older opponent. For just a flash, he could see . . . *something*—himself, charging at Stick, expecting a countermove. But Stick stood still, doing nothing, unnerving in his composure. Kirigi saw himself try again, with the same results.

He gave up and smiled coldly instead. "Hard to read the thoughts from blind eyes."

But Stick only stared off into nothingness. "Sight is overrated," he said softly. *"Listen."*

On the ground, Elektra's eyelids fluttered as she struggled to breathe. Her vision was muddled, filled with leaves and tree branches and . . . white things, scampering through the branches like nimble monkeys. No, not monkeys . . .

White-clad ninjas.

They swooped out of the trees like snow eagles, pulling Abby away before Kirigi and Typhoid could react. In a heartbeat Kirigi was surrounded, with no hope of winning the battle—Kinkou and Stone were dead; Tattoo was injured; Typhoid would never be a match for more than a few. It was best they retreat.

"Another day, old man," Kirigi spat, and then he was moving, too fast to follow. With Typhoid Mary and Tattoo right behind, he circled the tree in which Elektra had hidden herself. When he was just out of Stick's range of retaliation, Kirigi yanked free two of the *shuriken* Elektra had embedded in the tree and threw them with impossible-to-follow speed and aim. The deadly projectiles skimmed through the air and sliced through trees and leaves with ease, but Stick literally *heard* the air parting as they traveled. He whirled and brought up his walking stick, feeling it tremble as one of them hit it with vicious strength. He smiled as a spot of blood blossomed on his gray shirt. The other throwing star had found its mark, but the wound was easy to conceal—a tug on his jacket and no one knew the difference. Kirigi had impressive skill and sometimes, when the nights were quiet and long, Stick wondered how things would have turned out if the boy had been *his* student instead of the Hand's.

Stick motioned at Mark, and the younger man obediently lifted Elektra in his arms and, with his daughter watching behind them, carried her out of the forest after the blind man.

16

ELEKTRA SAW THE SKY, AND THE TREES, AND THE clouds. There was sun, too, but it kept fading in and out, lost behind huge gray and black thunderheads that swept in from nowhere to blot out the light. Maybe she was dreaming, or—

"Is she going to die?"

—already dead, because she kept seeing Stick's face superimposed over it all but through a sort of watery vapor. His image wavered in and out of her consciousness like a weak ghost, a specter that couldn't quite hang on to this reality. Most of the time she had her eyes closed, losing herself in the volcanic heat that surrounded everything that she was and would ever be. It was like lava running through her veins and her head, and oh, she thought she would sell her soul and everything she was for just a cold, cold shower and, maybe, a tall, bottomless glass of ice water.

"I don't know. A body can't be brought back twice."

A body? Whose body? And brought back from where? She had to be alive—she was certain that dead people didn't hear voices, didn't have thoughts, even the disjointed ones floating around in her consciousness. Hadn't she been dead once? Yes, she had, and she had felt nothing—it was just blackness, an eternal sleep where the foreverness of one's state of being is all and nothing, incomprehensible, nonsensical. This, then, could not be death—

"*If she leaves this time, she won't be back.*"

Was she leaving? She must be, because she was alive, and dead people don't go anywhere. Where was she going, and who was saying that? Her father? Matt? No, wait—it was Bullseye, that vicious Irishman who had tried to eviscerate her with her own sai—

He smiles blackly at her from only inches away and she can see the indentation of scar tissue on his forehead, that strange self-made target pattern. Already in pain, she has a moment—only that—to think about how she would so like to take a weapon and push it through the center of that scar, then he rams the sai into her stomach and drives it upward, pushing and pushing until it parts blood and organs and tissue and bone and finally breaks through the leather of her top. There is nothing in the world as it happens except for that core of complete and utter torture, and she feels every centimeter of the blade as it goes through—

The ambulance screams through the night, but she can't hear the sirens, can't even hear the paramedics even though one is leaning directly over her and telling her something. Then her hearing abruptly comes back, but it's choppy, and while she can hear him, the sound cuts in and out, like an old record skipping on a turntable. His voice is filled with urgency and he calls out something to the other one in the back—"Clear!"—then light hammers through her body, filling her up with heat. The hollow heaviness inside her chest heaves and stutters, then returns to that same choking emptiness. The light fills her again, more heat on top of the heat in the center of her body, more wasted effort to make that silent, still muscle in her chest wake up. The light comes a final, useless time—

Elektra sees her mother on the bed, lying there motionless and serene, while a white-coated man, the coroner called by the police, bends over her and scribbles on his clipboard. The blood surrounding her is . . . different this time, not so red, duller and drained of color. Her father stands at the window and stares outward as though he is searching for someone or something; his face is drawn and helpless, eyes ringed with purplish shadows. Elektra hears a sound behind her and she turns back toward the bed, just in time to see the coroner jerk his arms outward. The movement sends a white sheet billowing outward and it settles over her mother's form, and then another one floats downward, and another, and another, like gently falling snow. The child-sized version of herself walks over and takes the necklace, reaching beneath the layers of white, and then she turns and screams as a demon shrieks at her from the window, screams and screams and screams—

Elektra sat up, gasping and sweating.

A nightmare, that's all, just old, bad memories all

mixed up and boiling in her mind. The ones that never seemed to go away, no matter how hard she worked to keep them buried.

Where was she?

She was in bed, but not hers. The sheets—no blankets—were all startling white with no frills, very much like a hospital's. Elektra realized her hands were clenched into fists around the top sheet and she forced her fingers to let go so she could scrub at her face. When she did, her fingers came away slick with perspiration and slightly oily, evidence that she'd been lying here for a while. Her hair was tangled and lank, her bedclothes—more plain white, a long sleep shirt that she was already finding way too warm—were wet and stuck to her skin.

She peered around but there wasn't much to see. The one-window room was just as plain as the sheets— the window had a light-block shade and there was nothing on the walls above the two other pieces of furniture, a small table and a straight-backed chair. It took her a few seconds to focus, but Elektra could finally make out her own clothes, folded neatly, lying next to both of her sais. She could see from her position on the bed that the broken one had been expertly repaired.

Typhoid Mary—yes, now she remembered. Elektra looked down at her hands, then turned them over and flexed the fingers. There was no dirt under the fingernails or bruises on her knuckles. The rest of her body was the same, no cuts, bumps, or scrapes, so she must have been here—wherever *here* was—for some time while she healed. The memory of Stone tossing her through the air as though she weighed no more than a beach ball was still vivid, and that should have left her black and blue for a couple of weeks, but when she ran her fingers experimentally over her lower back . . . nothing. She thought she remembered Stick, but that couldn't be right; that recollection was probably nothing more than a hallucination brought on by the typhoid fever that had rampaged through her body. She was lucky to have survived—most people would've been worm food by now.

Moving carefully, Elektra brought her legs to the side of the bed and tested them, making sure she was strong enough to carry her own weight before trying to stand. She could, but she was going to have to go at it slowly—her muscles were weak from disuse and the sickness, her balance shaky. When she felt confident enough to try, she made her way carefully across the small room to the door on the other side. When she twisted the knob and pushed it open, it only took a glance to know exactly where she was.

Elektra stared outside for a few moments, taking it all in. Finally she closed the door and worked her way over to the small table and her pile of clean clothes.

She would *make* her body recover, *make* her muscles and stamina return, even if she had to do it by sheer force of will. She'd rested enough.

It was time to get dressed and return, once more, to the living.

It felt like a hundred years since Elektra had been at the camp, but the humiliation of having Stick kick her out so long ago was as fresh today as if it had happened yesterday. It didn't help that many of the instructors were still there, and every single one who saw her, of course, recognized her instantly. At least the students had all rotated out, the ones she'd trained with and bested gone on to whatever assignments the Chaste had seen fit to give them.

But her former embarrassment wasn't important now, and as she stood next to her mentor and watched Abby train in the same classes that she herself had trained in years ago, Elektra couldn't help feeling a mixture of pride and jealousy. The young girl was a natural, as much or more so than Elektra herself had been, slipping and ducking and parrying in the sparring class as though she had been in this class for years and should be teaching it rather than learning in it. Therein was the difference—Abby had, perhaps, a touch of Elektra's arrogance, but none of her anger. Elektra had never possessed the patience to mentor anyone else, but someday Abby would make an excellent instructor.

As Elektra watched, Abby finished with her sparring lesson and moved immediately to join a group of students practicing with *Rokshaku-bos*—bo staffs. Abby was the youngest in the group, and clearly the most talented; she moved effortlessly, anticipating every blow, feint, and parry. Elektra well remembered wearing the same uniform, a light-colored gi made of a gauzy fabric that was so lightweight it felt like you were wearing nothing at all. With Abby's hair dyed the same color as Elektra's, the teenager lacked only the headband that Elektra had used to keep her thick hair out of her face; she had no doubt that if Abby had known about that, the girl would have included that in her emulation of Elektra as well.

The class was an enjoyable thing to watch, and when Stick stepped into the middle of the students and brought them to a halt, it brought Elektra a faint, almost aching feeling of wanting to join in. "Don't look for your opponent," he told the students. "Know where he is. I'm blind and I can see more than any of you. Because I *don't* look."

He stepped out of the circle and the practicing began again. Elektra couldn't help admiring Abby above everyone else in the class—she could see the girl's level of combat and competence rise immediately. She stepped up behind Stick and spoke, not expecting to startle him. She didn't.

"You tell her, she gets it right away," Elektra said.

Stick nodded. "She can listen." He paused, then added, "It was the one gift you lacked."

Elektra didn't answer. What was there to say? He didn't need her to tell him he was right—he already knew that. They both did. They kept watching, and Elektra again had that feeling of enviousness about the teenager's incredible abilities. After another moment, he said, "She's everything they say."

Elektra sucked in her breath as her mind ticked away at the facts, sliding them into place like one of those old-fashioned car puzzles, the tiny ones with plastic squares that kept the kids occupied in the back seat. The answer had been there the entire time, but realizing it still left her more than a little stunned. "This whole war with the Hand," she said softly, "it's all about her, isn't it?"

Stick didn't say anything for a moment, but finally he answered. "They call her 'the treasure.' She was a prodigy from four or five. Her father had those martial arts schools, and word got around fast." Stick shifted his weight and tilted his head slightly, and Elektra knew he was still monitoring the class even as he was talking to her. "The Hand wanted her for themselves. They tried to steal her, but her father took her and fled."

"So when Mark refused," Elektra put in, "they decided to make sure no one else would get her."

Stick nodded and they stood together in silence for a

few minutes. Finally, Elektra asked the biggest question that had been plaguing her. That it came out from between her grinding teeth was unavoidable. "You hired me, didn't you? The contract with McCabe—you set all this up." Stick turned toward her, a look of surprise on his face, but Elektra was not deceived—she knew him too well, knew the expression he would use if he were feigning something. "The Hand has killers of its own, and who else would care? Except you."

A reluctant smile played across the older man's mouth as he relaxed. "Some people need to figure the way out for themselves. Your mind is more agile than it once was."

She wanted to be angry, but she was too tired for that. Not just from her bout with typhoid fever, but from all of it—the running, the killing, the deception. The . . . *loss*. "You knew I wouldn't kill them," she said in a low voice, "a girl and her father."

Stick only gave her an enigmatic glance. "Did I?"

Her eyes widened and she scowled. "It was a test, Stick. It was *all* a test, wasn't it? From the day you threw me out of here."

That same knowing smile slipped across Stick's face. "I knew what you would do. I just wanted to make you *do* it. The decency of your soul has always embarrassed you." She let an unladylike snort evidence her skepticism, but Stick only gave her a mocking laugh in return. "There are some lessons that can't be taught,

Elektra. They must be lived to be understood. When you came to me, you were boiling over with anger. Whatever grace you once had was squeezed out of you by violence and tragedy. This is not the way. It is not our way.

She pressed her lips together. "You always talk in riddles, Stick."

His unseeing eyes gazed at the students going through their lessons. "Yes, I've heard that before. It keeps my students from getting lazy."

Elektra folded her arms and turned to face him. He didn't bother to do the same, preferring to remain in place and monitor Abby's class. Despite her exhaustion and the smile that wanted to materialize at Stick's rare self-humor, she couldn't help feeling a tiny flare of the old anger. She hadn't seen his body, but she knew Mc-Cabe had died because of his efforts at protecting her, Abby, and Mark—died because of Stick's perpetual game playing. And he had almost not been the only one. "What if the Hand had killed me? And her?"

Stick didn't even move a muscle. "It was a chance I was willing to take. Anyway, I had faith in your abilities."

Elektra stared at him, trying to find her way through her own conflicting feelings. Praise was something she seldom got, and certainly not from the mentor she'd adored but who had rejected her years ago. Most of the time she'd rather fight, but . . . "It's not my war,

Stick," she said aloud. "You had no right to drag me into this."

Now he did move, swiveling only his head in her direction. "I drag in who I want," he said flatly. "Who I *need*."

She ground her teeth. "And now you're dragging in Abby."

Now Stick shrugged. "As long as Kirigi's alive, she's only safe here anyway. She's got no choice."

"And no freedom," Elektra muttered. But really, what was there left to say? He was right, so she finally just turned and walked away. There were no more arguments about it—as so often happened with life, it was what it was. This situation with Kirigi had to be resolved or Abby, and Mark, would never be safe. Was it better to be safe and restricted, or doomed and free? She already knew the answer.

She wandered the camp, going through the old haunts and training areas, places that she hadn't thought about in years. A glance in one direction showed her a bandaged-up Mark headed her way on what was no doubt a physical therapy outing; he was balancing on a crutch and limping, concentrating on the ground and where he was walking as he moved forward with a teeth-gritting determination. He raised his head and caught her eye, then smiled and started toward her, but Elektra intentionally turned her back and went the other way. She needed to be alone so she could think about things, about Abby and Mark, about herself . . . and all their places in this crazy, mixed-up world. There was all the deception, too, that had gone around and twisted up her life, getting her involved in things she was never meant to take on. With all that on her mind, Elektra sure didn't need Mark Miller around, mixing up her thoughts even more.

Kirigi waited impatiently next to Tattoo, unable to stop himself from shifting from foot to foot. The tattoo-covered man was standing silently next to him, head thrown back and eyes only half open; his mouth was slightly slack as he concentrated, working to keep in sync with the hawk's rapid-fire movements and human brain–enhanced perceptions. Finally the creature returned to its master, circling the sky to pinpoint Tattoo, then plummeting straight down and slamming into his arm. Tattoo came back to himself with a jerk, then grimaced and rubbed his arm; where the bird had reintegrated itself, the flesh was a fiery red, like a second-degree burn. That coloration would be gone in two more minutes, as would the sting of the bird's homecoming. Of all the creatures inked on Tattoo's body, this one liked to come back with a bang, diving to "Daddy" as though it were attacking prey.

"What do you know?" Kirigi demanded.

"There is much tension between the blind man and Elektra," Tattoo told him.

Kirigi digested this. "The assassin is the girl's last hope, so I want to know where she is at all times. And we must kill Elektra. *Tonight*."

Tattoo nodded, then took another deep inhalation. A moment later his head fell back and his eyes glazed, and once again the hawk ripped itself free of his flesh and soared into the sky.

17

Elektra knew Abby was inside her cabin before she even stepped onto the porch.

She kept up her measured pace, never slowing until she climbed the steps, turned the knob, and pushed inside. There was the girl, all right, standing in the middle of the floor and playing with Elektra's sais, swiping them through the air with practiced, fluid moves that followed first the *lamenco* pattern, then the *doce pares* pattern, executing both with admirable precision even if she was using the wrong weapons for the drills. Elektra watched her for a second, then said, "Still breaking and entering, I see."

Abby froze in the middle of a double *oradabi* strike, then lowered the sais and gave Elektra a sheepish look. "Sorry."

Elektra shrugged and sat on the edge of the bed. "Forget it. It's a talent in the shadow arts. Keep practicing—you'll need it."

Abby came forward hesitantly, as if she were going to sit next to her, but Elektra stood before the girl had the chance. She started pacing back and forth, measuring out the length of the small cabin, then turning back.

Finally Abby spoke. "I'm sorry I lied to you."

"Don't apologize," Elektra said shortly. Her stride quickened without her realizing it.

Abby nodded, but her expression said she didn't believe Elektra, so she kept talking. "I didn't want to lie. My dad didn't either. It made me sick not to tell you, I swear."

Elektra frowned and kept going, back and forth, back and forth. "We all lie, okay? None of us tell the truth about ourselves."

"Including you," noted Abby.

"Especially me."

Abby tilted her head thoughtfully. "You mean like the whole killing people for money thing."

Elektra nodded without slowing. "That . . . sure."

Abby watched her for a moment more, then said, "And the counting."

This time Elektra did stop. "Excuse me?"

Abby nodded. "Like when I was counting windows because I'm a little obsessive-compulsive? So are you."

"No, I'm . . ." Elektra started to say, then her voice trailed off. "I used to be. I used to count . . . when I was a kid. But I haven't done it in years."

"You were doing it just now," Abby insisted. "When you walk like that, what're you doing?"

Elektra's frowned deepened. "I'm just . . . pacing. It helps me think."

"Yeah?" Abby smirked, then pranced across the room, doing an exaggerated version of Elektra's walk. "One . . . two . . . three . . . *skip*. One . . ." The assassin flushed with embarrassment and aggravation, more at being humiliated than being called out on something that turned out to be true. Honesty she could take, but not ridicule. "You're counting your steps," Abby continued smugly. "To control your bad thoughts."

Elektra's eyes narrowed. "Don't mock me, Abby. I'm your superior."

Now the teenager laughed outright. "My *what?*"

Up to now, Elektra had simply been holding the girl to warrior etiquette—not to mention courtesy and good manners—but Abby's flippancy was fast sending her into the realm of irritation. "As a warrior," she told her coldly, "I'm your superior. Even if I do *count.*"

But Abby only gave her a careless shrug. "Maybe."

Elektra arched one eyebrow. "Maybe? Would you like to find out for sure?"

This time the teenager outright snorted. "I'm going to go look for my dad," she said sullenly. It was obvious she didn't like being told what to do by Elektra, and definitely didn't agree with the notion that the older woman was better at anything than her. She went to the door and Elektra turned away, ready to let the whole thing blow over. Then, without warning, Abby shot out a reverse kick.

She had thought she would catch Elektra by surprise, show her just how knowledgeable she was and how quickly she was picking up her lessons. That would show Elektra that she didn't know everything, that—

Elektra swept Abby's kick to the side without even looking behind her. Then she leaned slightly forward and swung her own leg hard into Abby's, taking the girl neatly off her feet.

Still, even if she wasn't anticipating it, Abby was good; instead of falling, the teen rolled into a cartwheel, then came back after Elektra, launching blow after blow, each of which Elektra blocked, slipped, or parried effortlessly. It wasn't until the girl's back bumped the wall that she realized she'd been slowly forced backward, that it was Elektra, not she, who was in total control of this battle, and the woman wasn't even breathing hard. Feeling trapped, Abby upped her offensive, her punches and backfists coming faster and faster.

"Don't force it," Elektra said calmly. Her eyes were half closed and she looked infuriatingly serene. "Relax and let it flow. Stay focused."

But there was more at stake here than just a lesson— in Abby's mind she had something to prove, a sort of self-ranking in the eyes of this woman she so admired. She shot out with a hard punch—

Elektra scooped her fist, then delivered a stinging, pride-crushing slap to Abby's face.

It hurt—well, not much—but it was *so* embarrassing. Totally enraged now, Abby stepped up her attack even more, becoming more and more frustrated as she realized subconsciously that the harder *she* tried, the less energy Elektra had to use to defend against her. She felt like an idiot but she seemed unable to stop herself, like a kitten jumping up and down in a sort of shadow art rope-a-dope game, and it was a pitiably short time before Abby was panting and sweating and barely able to remember any of the training camp lessons she'd learned so far.

And, as any good assassin would, Elektra moved in to take advantage of her target's weakness.

She turned the tables, going smoothly from defense to offense, slipping into a level of Jeet Kune Do so advanced that Abby hadn't even come close to training in it. Abby barely managed to block the first of Elektra's strikes, then she lost it altogether—she missed first one, then another, taking light, humiliating blows on the side of her head and in her rib cage, shoulders, arms, and more, some of which she had no idea could have killed her had Elektra not controlled her force. Finally, Abby simply surrendered and collapsed to the floor, tears running down her face.

Elektra let her cry for a moment, then her stone face softened and she pulled Abby upright and sat her on the edge of the bed. She sat next to the girl and, when Abby's tears went into full sobs, she held her while the girl cried against her chest for a long, long time, stroking her hair and not saying anything through the tears, trying to make herself *not* count as she rocked Abby back and forth. After a while, she said the only thing she thought might comfort Abby. "You'll be better than I am. Very soon."

Instead of helping, it only made the teenager cry harder. "I don't want to stay here—I'm just a kid!" Elektra didn't know whether to laugh or shake her head at that, and Abby sobbed again. "I started doing this for fun, and now people want to kill me because I'm good at it? What's up with *that?*" Her chest hitched as she tried to laugh at the ridiculousness of the whole situation, but she was still too upset. There was nowhere else in the world that would make her feel better than to be with Elektra right now, so she wrapped her arms around the assassin's neck and held on for all she was worth. Elektra didn't fight it, just let the girl hang on, held her back, and let her mind mull over the dangers she knew had to be headed their way.

Neither Elektra nor Abby saw the larger-than-life spider that pulled itself from the colorful material of the jacket Abby had tossed on the end of the table, and cautiously crawled away.

*   *   *

Elektra watched Abby sleep and thought how young she looked right now, innocent and childlike. Her eyelids were a little swollen and her nose was red from the crying; she'd fallen asleep on Elektra's bed about a half hour ago, and from Elektra's vantage point it almost looked like Abby was sucking her thumb. But it was just an illusion, the angle of her face; Abby was on her way to growing up, and maybe a little . . . no, a *lot* faster than she should have to.

Yeah, it was time to take care of this.

Moving in total silence, Elektra found her case— Stick had sent someone to retrieve it from McCabe's after they were sure that Kirigi wasn't monitoring it— and changed her clothes, feeling more comfortable than she had in weeks now that she had her familiar red leather costume back on. Sais in hand, she sent Abby a last, almost maternal look, then slipped out of the cabin and into the growing dusk, carefully pulling the door closed behind her. The students had long ago dispersed from training; now they were eating their evening meal and preparing for the nightly shower and meditation. The shadows were growing long and silent as Elektra left the compound. No one saw her . . .

. . . except Abby, who had sensed Elektra's absence the instant the assassin had stepped out the cabin door. Abby had her shoes on and was out the door within seconds, never losing sight of the woman in red as she strode across the grounds of the training camp.

And the spider watched them both from its hiding place beneath the table.

Dropping from a long, silken thread, the spider seemingly came out of nowhere to land on Tattoo's shoulder, then it scuttled across his collarbone and worked its way into its proper place on Tattoo's neck. After a long moment, Tattoo opened his eyes and lifted his head. "The girl's left the cabin."

Pleased for the first time since their defeat in the woods, Kirigi smiled, then nodded to the others. They rose and followed him out the door, ready to finally finish the job of eliminating Elektra and the treasure.

18

THE DARKNESS SURROUNDED ELEKTRA LIKE A COM-
forting cloak, concealing her movements and letting
her slip through across the full expanse of the compound and disappear into the trees. Even though the
camp was heavily guarded, she made sure no one noticed her—this was not the time to be stopped or have
to answer questions about her destination. The night
was perfect, and the heavy canopy of overhead leaves
kept even the moonlight from revealing her location.
She took an old path that hadn't been used in years—
perhaps the last person to walk this trail had been she
herself, when she'd last used it as a child. Even after so
many years, her feet found the way almost of their own
accord, stepping lightly and soundlessly through the
blackness, knowing where the dips in the ground were,
that spot where the old tree branch had grown up and
out of the soil, exposing itself as a tripping spot for the
unwary.

Moving through the dark was a little like trusting
your instincts to move you through a time tunnel—
Elektra wasn't sure how long she walked, but she knew

it was the right amount of time and that it would take her to exactly the place she wanted to go. Eventually the path followed around and broke at the edge of a lawn, or at least what was left of it after all these years. Now it was more like a clearing on its way to being overgrown. It was filled with weeds and small trees, the precursors to what would someday become just another part of the forest if she didn't do something to stop it and save the family estate that still belonged to her. She probably never would.

The end of the path joined the driveway, now pitted and cracked by the sun, dissolving at the edges as the grass and weeds claimed a little more of the asphalt each year. There was no tree cover here and the moon was full and strong, a natural illuminator. Elektra followed the drive all the way up to the ornate iron gate; it looked different now that the years had etched its pattern in a coating of rust that the light of the moon made look like dried blood. Atop the gate in stylized wrought iron was the oversized family letter, just as she remembered. The last time she'd left this place, her father's driver had stopped on the outside and padlocked the gate shut; that same old lock was still there and still holding, but it was rusty and gave easily enough beneath the blade of one sai.

Elektra followed the inner driveway to the double doors beneath the wide portico. The doors were weathered and cracking, just like the driveway, and the paint on the line of once-white columns that stretched to either side of the front porch was peeling away, exposing an underside that had gone gray and black with mildew. Elektra stood there for a moment and listened to the night, then finally pulled out the chain around her neck. At the end of it, next to the ankh that had belonged to her dead mother, was the house key she had never thrown away. It went into the lock and turned with surprising smoothness, as though of all things destiny and the universe had thrown at her, in this one realm, this thing that Elektra *must* do, it would allow nothing to stand in her way.

The door swung open on cranky, grating hinges, and she stepped into the oversized foyer. It was like a tomb tiled in dusty black and white; no footprints marred the layer of gray on the floor—no one had been in here at all, not since her father had closed up the house after her mother's death and relocated the both of them to New York. As Elektra moved through the house, she found the same thick coating of time draped over all the dust coverings protecting the furniture; here and there cobwebs hung in the air, so heavy with the gray dust that they waved in the drafty air like the tattered remains of ancient lace curtains.

She went all the way through the mansion, back to the far wall of the rear sitting room. That wall had floor-to-ceiling windows hung with thick, burgundy-colored drapes; their color had gone gray with time and yanking them open sent a cloud of pale dirt into the air. The windows behind them were also grimy, but not so bad that Elektra couldn't see through the glass, across the expanse of the drained and covered Olympic-sized swimming pool to the stone pool house she had known so well. Looking at it like that, through the sitting room window, was like opening a fountain of youth and pouring out all her childhood memories to be relived all over again.

She prances across the lawn in her new summer dress, the one her mother had the seamstress at Nieman Marcus custom make just for her. It's yellow, bright and cheerful, but the best part is the spray of scarlet flowers down the full skirt . . . or maybe it's the hand-tatted lace ruffles sewn around the bottom hem . . . or even the way the front of it laces up like one of those Swedish milkmaid dresses. This is a great summer, the best she's ever had, with her mother and father happy and nothing in the world to worry about—

She executes perfect cartwheels, one after another, her feet landing surely on the grass again and again as her father watches with a smile on his face. His laughter is full and it rings in her ears as she performs for him—

The maze, her great and wonderful green hiding place, gives her up to her mother's knowing steps. She'd never been so happy as right now, as she and her mother play together in it. Her mother chases and finally catches her, tickling her until Elektra begs her to stop. The world flies by in flashes of blue sky and green leaves as her mother picks her up and twirls her, turning around and around and around—

And then, the demon—or is it a man?—slips out her mother's bedroom window . . .

If Elektra didn't want to talk to him, that was fine, Mark thought sourly. But he wanted to know where his daughter was, and to make sure she was all right. That she was probably in Elektra's cabin with her was just a coincidence, and he wasn't going to let Elektra's anger with him prevent him from keeping tabs on Abby.

As he hobbled up to the cabin door, Mark gritted his teeth against the aches down his legs and for the hundredth time wished he could have healed as quickly as Elektra had recovered from the typhoid fever. He looked around again, then frowned. The cabin was dark, but that didn't mean anything—Abby had fallen asleep in here before and stayed the night rather than find her way back to their own small place in the dark. He usually didn't mind, but . . . All right, fine—so he was going to use this as an excuse to face off with Elektra. It was about time.

He knocked on the door, then knocked again after a long few moments. Balancing on his crutch, Mark finally pushed the door open and swept the wall on his right until his fingers brushed the light switch. It flipped on and even though it was a low wattage bulb, the sudden glare against the blackness made him squint. When he could finally open them, he was facing nothing but an empty cabin with a neatly made bed in the center.

Where the hell was his daughter?

Stick's cabin was as dark as Elektra's had been, and at first, Mark thought the man wasn't there. But no—Stick didn't need lights to see, so why would he bother? When Mark knocked, Stick's voice answered immediately, and Mark just had to deal with the fact that he was going to be holding a conversation in an utterly dark room.

"They're gone," Mark announced. He stepped through the open door then felt his way in as far as he dared. There wasn't any sense in being delicate. "Both of them."

He had to strain his eyes to make out the movement, but he finally saw Stick nodding. The older man was sitting on a straight-back chair with his hands folded on his lap, as calm as Mark was frantic. "I told Abby not to go," Stick said, more to himself than Mark. "She is as willful as Elektra." He inclined his head and for the first time, Mark noticed a green-clad ninja standing silently against the far wall. The man had nearly blended in with the shadows. "We should ready the men."

"Go?" Mark demanded. "Go *where?*" He couldn't stop himself from emphasizing his question with a thump on the floor with the end of his crutch.

"Elektra has left the compound," Stick responded with that same damnable tranquility. "I presume, to draw Kirigi's hand. Your daughter has followed her."

Mark stared at him in astonishment, but that rapidly gave way to fear. Abby might think she was tough, but she was nowhere near ready to face off against people like Kirigi and his thugs. "*What?* Then what are we doing here—we have to go after them! *Now,* old man!"

But Stick only stared blandly at him, and both he and Mark knew it would do no good to threaten him. "Mr. Miller," Stick said patiently, "we will go as quickly as we can, but you are in no condition to fight . . . and you never will be. As for Abby . . . you must accept that your daughter is becoming a warrior."

"She's thirteen years old!" Mark said loudly. He couldn't seem to control his voice. "She's—"

"She is strong," Stick interrupted. "And so is Elektra. Put your faith in them."

This time, Mark *did* grab at Stick, gripping his upper arm the way a drowning man snatches at a rope hanging from the side of a boat. As much as he wanted to hold on, when Stick swiveled his head in Mark's direction and fixed that endless blue stare on him, Mark knew he had no choice but to quietly let him go.

"God, you're a cold bastard," he said thickly.

"I suppose," Stick replied, but he was anything but affected by Mark's proclamation.

Churning with frustration, Mark swung around and hobbled toward the door.

"You're too late," Stick said from behind him. "*It's already started.*"

But Mark, of course, had no choice but to keep going.

Elektra had stayed in the rear sitting room, looking out at the abandoned pool and the pool house as she first mulled over her childhood memories, then went into a cleansing, calming meditative state. While she might want to remember only the happy memories—except for her mother's death, of course—her life in this house had been a mixed blessing. Even so, it had been the only place where she'd had an existence with both parents at once, and that made the time most special and irreplaceable in her mind. Because of that, it was here that she would make her stand—and she was well aware that it might be her last—against Kirigi and whatever other evil he would bring with him. She would honor her mother and father, and their memories, by destroying the worst of those in this world, men—and women—just like the ones who had murdered each of them.

The fine, tiny hairs along the back of her neck suddenly rippled. Elektra tensed and her eyes narrowed as she saw the shadow of a hawk glide past on the other side of the window—danger was close, and she was clearly being watched. The seconds ticked by and one by one, she forced her muscles to relax. Then, lit only by the moonlight, she rose and moved into the hall. But she did not hurry.

She was not afraid.

In the kitchen, she rummaged silently through the drawers until she found the one that held the emergency candles and matches. She lit one, then went back to the stove closer to the living room's entrance, knowing her plan would only work if there was still fuel left in the propane tanks. Twisting all six of the knobs on the old chef's range, she held her breath, waiting . . . then smiled slightly as she heard the faintest of hissing sounds. A few seconds later, she smelled gas. It wouldn't be long now until she left her father's estate behind for good, and there was no more time for goodbyes or fond memories.

She was right. There was barely enough time for the gas to build up enough in the air when suddenly all the windows in the kitchen shattered inward. Glass shards crisscrossed the room, turning it into a swirling zone of danger, but that meant nothing to the dozen or more black-garbed ninjas who poured through the ragged edges of the windows.

Elektra never gave them the chance to get close to her. At the same time she vaulted through the living door, she flung the candle toward the stove. She had a tense two seconds when, as the candle tumbled through the air, she thought the flame might go out—if that happened, she had little chance of surviving the next few minutes.

BOOM!

Shadow-black bodies went in every direction as the stove exploded, destroyed the kitchen and everything in it. An instant later, a gout of billowing acrid green smoke that proved their deaths joined the dust, debris and smoke from the fire now consuming what was left of the room.

Elektra glanced back before melting into the darkness of the living room. At the cost of her family home, she'd won the fight—

For now.

The silence of the night disintegrated into a scream of glass and fire. Kirigi, Tattoo, and Typhoid jerked in surprise, then stared at the far end of the house, where orange flames mixed with the telltale death smoke—so much for his ninjas. He'd probably been foolish to think they could take on Elektra anyway, but why waste his own energy if she was idiot enough to make a

243

mistake? Still, he couldn't help smiling in admiration; once again the gaijin had proven her wisdom in the shadow arts.

"Clever girl," Kirigi said.

And with that, he turned and stepped into the darker shadow thrown by one of the massive trees that dotted the overgrown front lawn.

And literally disappeared.

19

SOMEONE WAS IN THE LIVING ROOM WITH HER.

The air was tinged with smoke from the kitchen fire, but so far the flames had kept to the kitchen and the more readily consumed mahogany cabinets. Now the fine hairs on the back of Elektra's neck rose for a second time, and her watering eyes narrowed to slits as she tried to focus in the smoky darkness. Here and there the covered furniture appeared as lighter clumps, but beyond the lazily floating smoke haze, Elektra could see nothing, no movement, nothing amiss. Finally she stopped, then started to lower herself into a crouch and—

A wind came out of nowhere, cold and hard enough to rip the dusty sheets free of the furniture and chase away the layers of smoke. The sheets whirled around her, flapping and shifting, surrounding her like wild, white ghosts and creating more shadows with their movement, exposing the darker furniture beneath them and making more places that she had to try and keep track of.

"Your skills are impressive."

She spun at the sound of Kirigi's voice, trying to locate him. There—standing behind the second floor bannister midway between the curving stairs and where the hallway disappeared into the bedrooms beyond. His slender figure disappeared and reappeared as those damnable sheets swung and spun over her head. Suddenly he jumped nimbly over the bannister and dropped toward her.

Elektra had her sais out instantly to slash at the air and the sheets, but Kirigi landed a good twelve feet away. He turned to face her as she started toward him, but he only sneered at her derisively. *"But incomplete,"* he whispered in an echoing tone, and then she lost sight of him completely.

She went back toward the floor, lowered her body until it she was nearly crawling across the musty carpeting, seeing Kirigi's face shift in and out of the sheets still rippling in the air, driven by a wind that would not stop. Her intermittent strikes were useless—he was always somewhere else by the time her blade parted the white fabric.

"Your powers are useless against me," she heard him say, but his voice sounded like it was coming from anywhere and everywhere at once and damn it, she just couldn't *get* him.

There was only one way to deal with this.

Knowing it was a dangerous, desperate move, Elektra shut her eyes.

The living room is a fractured and incomprehensible box in her vision, obscured and blurry with moving white shapes. Kirigi swings his katanas through the fluttering sheets—

She opened her eyes, but everything around her still looked like the same thing, a sea of drifting wings, the flapping of a hundred huge birds. Uncertain, Elektra lunged toward the closest one, slicing at the fabric with her sais. It looked as though it had a human form concealed within it, but her blade found nothing hidden in its folds but air.

Her kimagure was useless here—the sheets made everything in the room look the same, and while Kirigi *was* in here somewhere, it was impossible for her mind's vision to successfully show her where.

"A student strikes a blow," Kirigi said. Once more he sounded like he was everywhere, but common sense and methodology dictated that he would be moving ever closer, inching toward her and looking for that killing stroke. Wouldn't it come from behind her, where his position would be the safest and have the most stealth? Elektra spun and arced her weapons in a double line through the sheet behind her; they fluttered to the floor in evenly spaced ribbons, but again— nothing.

"A teacher anticipates the strike," Kirigi said softly, "and blocks it."

Another one of the sheets slithered in front of her,

this time wrapping around one arm and her neck, sliding across her face. Elektra had to force herself not to flail at them, to maintain her control and discipline.

Kirigi's voice came again. "A *master* anticipates the block . . . and does the unexpected."

The sheets fluttered faster around her, suspended in the air as they twisted and turned as though they were living creatures. The faster they spun, the more shadows they created, the more tension they built, the more Elektra's nerves screamed.

"A master's attack cannot be foreseen."

Elektra gasped as one of the sheets whipped around her head without warning. A flick of her wrist sliced through it, but the ends of still more of them snapped at her like wet towels, leaving little red welts across her skin and forcing her to fight the sheets as though they were the opponent rather than the living, breathing man who was controlling them.

Kirigi's taunting laughter echoed around the room and Elektra ground her teeth, reminding herself not to let him get to her, commanding her mind to stay focused. He was toying with her now, mocking her by slapping the sheets against her face, then using his katanas to slice them away. The pieces of fabric writhed and jumping in humanlike forms, tricking her eyes and sabotaging her judgment.

Enough—she was through playing little man-ego games. She let herself shift into instinct, then whirled sharply in a different direction, letting her body find its own way when her mind might have told her something else. In a split second she came up and sliced viciously at a sheet directly in front of her.

Finally, she faced Kirigi.

He was standing at the foot of the stairs, calm and relaxed. Elektra slashed at him quickly with her sais, but he was too fast—he met her strokes with his katanas and, to her dismay, literally sliced off the tips of both of her weapons.

When he spoke, at least now Elektra knew where he was. "Your blades are not strong enough," he said scornfully, "because *you* are not strong enough." Before she could retort, her sais were gone entirely, knocked out of her hands and spinning away across the dark floor as she blinked. Kirigi grinned at her evilly.

"Thanks for the lesson."

Both Elektra and Kirigi started and turned at the sound of Abby's voice. The girl stood, smiling congenially not three feet away, and Elektra had just enough time to be alarmed before Abby charged Kirigi. The necklace and bracelet were gone, traded in for a genuine and quite deadly pair of kusari-fundos that spiraled through the air with dazzling speed.

Even so, Kirigi sidestepped Abby's attack with a speed of his own that was nothing less than incredible, and while Elektra was still shocked to see Abby, Kirigi was clearly delighted. "Brave girl," he practically purred. He smile was absolutely hellish. "You taught her well."

Oh no—Elektra had not come out here to battle Kirigi just so he could murder Abby. She leapt toward him, but he ducked and countered with a graceful but powerful uppercut that sent her sprawling. The sheets still streaming around the room suddenly exploded with movement, whipping into a frenzy and knocking Abby flat. Down on her knees, the girl tried to crawl away from them, but they buried her and Elektra.

And finally, all was quiet.

Kirigi stood in the center of the room, surrounded by white debris and shredded pieces of fabric. Elektra lay somewhere beneath the jumbled piles of white, unmoving and silent, but Abby threw off the material covering her and rose.

"But now," Kirigi told her, "it's time for a new master."

Looking more serene than she felt—she was terrified—Abby brought up her chains and spun them, but every time she struck at Kirigi he easily deflected her blows, retaliating with strikes of his own that forced her to slowly go on the defensive. She backed away, unwillingly allowing him to guide her across the room, remembering only too well Elektra's previous lesson against allowing herself to become trapped but helpless to stop it from happening again.

Kirigi advanced again, but this time Abby saw something move within the sheets on the floor behind him. She kept blocking his strikes and inching backward, still searching for that elusive opportunity to sidestep on her own and wrap a chain—or both—around his hands so she could relieve him of those katanas. In another two seconds, Elektra soundlessly eased aside the last sheet covering her, then sprinted for the staircase. She and Abby locked gazes, and before Kirigi realized what was going to happen, Abby went on the offensive one last time. The attack took Kirigi by surprise—he didn't give up his ground, but for once he wasn't forcing Abby backward, either. At the highest arc of her strike, Abby twisted her wrist and whipped out with her arm—

—and let go of one end of the chain in her hand.

It soared up and over Kirigi's head and he automatically followed the movement, then scowled when he saw Elektra leaning over the bannister. The second he took his gaze off Abby, she sprang; Elektra caught the weighted end of the chain, wrapped it around her wrist, and *pulled*, jerking Abby up and swinging her out of Kirigi's range. Still hanging on to her end of the chain, Abby landed almost halfway up the staircase, and then Elektra had her safely—at least until Kirigi got his bearings again—on the second floor landing with her.

Elektra let go of the kusari-fundo, and Abby expertly reeled it back in. Then Elektra grabbed Abby by the arm and hauled her down the hallway, trying to put as much distance between them and Kirigi as she could. "Abby," she told her as she steered the girl through the doorway into the master suite. "You need to go—"

"I'm *not* leaving you!"

Before Elektra could retort, she saw Kirigi appear in the doorway to the room. There was no way to go but out, so Elektra lashed out at the window, smashing it with a vicious sidekick. "You're just like me," she complained. "A real pain in the ass!" Before Kirigi could get closer, both of them sprang out the window.

They landed easily on the soft grass and weeds below, both rolling back into a standing position and dashing away. As they fled, Elektra glanced back and saw Kirigi watching, unperturbed, from the window. Something passed overhead and Elektra's gaze snapped upward—it was that elusive hawk again, its shadow bisecting the light of the moon as it glided past.

A final glance over her shoulder at Kirigi's figure in the window, and it didn't make Elektra feel any better to see that he was smiling.

"They're coming."

Tattoo heard Master Kirigi's voice in his head as clearly as if the man had been standing next to him. He nodded and slipped off his robe, folding it quickly but still with ceremonial precision. His skin glistened with perspiration and movement, the slender, knotted muscles making the color-soaked tattoos pulsate across his flesh. Inked around his arms and acros

one of the more complex pieces of his
tricate meshing of arabesques and hi
the casual eye might mistake for noth
pretty design, but when someone looked
too closed his eyes and concentrated, and after a moment the pattern began to shiver, then twist. The
twisting increased, then his back bulged as the first of
hundreds of venomous snakes pulled free. Just as suddenly they transformed again, this time into thousands
of tiny, winking lights. They burst off his back like a
fireworks display and fell to the ground. A moment
later they streamed across the ground and toward the
bridge leading into the maze.

Abby and Elektra clambered over the bridge, no
longer trying to be stealthy. Up ahead, way too close for
comfort, they could see countless spots of light flooding
toward them like an eerily silent display of sparks. Elektra didn't know what they were, but she was sure of one
thing—she and Abby needed to avoid them. Getting
into the maze, *deep* into it, was their only hope to get
away from Kirigi—Tattoo was nearby and his master
would use him to find them and attack. Elektra had
seen Tattoo's weapons, but she also knew she probably
hadn't seen them all. The wise warrior would always
save the best and most deadly for the final kill. If nothing else, the trees planted precisely at each corner

253

he once-living puzzle would shield them from
ying eyes of anything the tattooed man could
d overhead.

Abby glanced behind them, then gasped and
clutched at Elektra's elbow. The assassin followed
Abby's pointing finger, then grimaced as she saw movement on the surface of the bridge—the lights, bursting
through the slats and cascading over the old wooden
railings. Elektra urged the girl to move faster, pulling at
her, but now the lights seemed to be everywhere, ex-
ploding from the hedges like crazily waving sparklers.
They swirled around and between Elektra and Abby,
trying to force them apart, but Elektra wasn't going to
let that happen. She sprinted toward the center of the
maze, using her childhood knowledge of the structure,
knowing where each corridor, turn, and dead end was
from the countless weeks and months she'd spent playing in it as a child. For a precious few seconds she
thought they had the upper hand, then she glanced
back—

—and realized Abby was gone.

Abby ran as fast as she could, but when she glanced
over her shoulder, all she could see was a sheet of
lights—it looked like thousands of them—coming
right for her. She gasped and surged forward, saw a
break in the hedge and turned right, then turned again.
Another turn and she made herself pause as it hit her

that she was not only running blindly, but she'd gotten separated from Elektra. She wanted to go back the way she'd come but she couldn't—there were the lights again, hurtling in her direction and—

No!

They weren't lights at all, but pinpoints of . . . what? Eyes? Maybe, but that didn't matter, because the lights were suddenly gone and in their place were *snakes*, hundreds of them, rushing at her down the pathway, churning out of the hedges surrounding her. She whirled and started to flee, but all she got for her effort was a face-full of hedge—she'd turned into a dead end! She was trapped, and with no way to escape, all Abby could do was flail wildly as the glittering scales of countless reptiles twined about her body and ultimately held her prisoner.

Elektra dashed back the way they'd come, hoping Abby had turned instinctively toward the house. As she made her way back through the maze, expertly negotiating the turns and twists into the shortest path possible, her heart hammered with fear for the teenager. Then she skidded around the last turn and jerked herself up short as her face twisted in rage.

There, only a few feet away, was Tattoo, the cause of a good chunk of her and Abby's misery. His skin was coated in a glowing, iridescent blue, and he was rising from a lotus position, holding his arms out in front of him like he was urging a herd of invisible beasts forward. He probably was, and no doubt they were descending upon Abby even as Elektra bared her teeth and stepped directly into his path.

The ink-covered killer was concentrating so deeply that he didn't even realize she'd stepped in front of him, and it could be only a bad thing that he was shaking and smiling despite his deep mind sink.

"Nice trick," Elektra said with all the sweetness she could manage. Tattoo's trembling stopped abruptly, and he opened one eye. The pupil rolled slightly as he tried to bring back only what he needed of his thoughts. Unlike his previous decisions, this would turn out to be a bad one, indeed. "But I've seen it before," Elektra added.

Before he could focus enough to move out of her range, Elektra stepped quickly into his opened arms and slid her right arm around his neck until her hand was flat against his cheekbone. Bracing herself against him, rib cage to rib cage, she snapped her left arm forward as hard as she could—

Crack!

Abby thrashed within the grip of the snakes, fighting desperately for freedom. She twisted, then turned in the other direction—

—and nearly fell flat on her face. Without warning, the reptiles holding her exploded outward, spewing nasty black fluid toward the maze as they released their hold. In a matter of seconds Abby was surrounded by small, dark puddles instead of the pulsing, twisting snakes. Finally, *finally*, she could breathe. Finally she could run.

Time to find Elektra.

Elektra stepped back as Tattoo slumped to the ground with a broken neck. An instant later, the ink patterns across his arms and chest bled messily out of his skin, sliding down his body like tears of oil.

Elektra gave a tight, grim smile. Abby should be safe . . .

At least for now.

20

Tattoo lay dead at her feet, but Elektra knew there was no time to celebrate. She headed back into the maze toward Abby, but this time her steps were a little more hesitant—she *thought* she knew which way to go, but it wasn't a matter of just finding her way through it—every decision had the potential to be devastating. The wind picked up and brought with it the unpleasant recollection of Kirigi's windstorm back at the house, and then something happened that took her anxiety level to a whole new height.

A single leaf blew in front of her.

It fluttered on the cool breeze, turning and twisting like a perfect example of nature suspended for her viewing. The only problem was that it was *dead*, unnaturally so, black and withered with the ends twisted in a way that could only mean one thing:

Typhoid Mary.

"She's here," Elektra breathed, and then more leaves suddenly blew into her path, dark evidence of the diseased woman's presence. She had to find Abby before it was too late.

She charged into the maze, taking turns and twists and letting her unconscious memory keep her from getting lost. That instinctive memory wouldn't help her locate Abby, though—the girl could be anywhere, although the dying sounds from Tattoo's herd just a few moments ago made Elektra believe the teenager had to be close. It was just a matter of finding the right pathway.

Abby heard Elektra's voice calling out, but the high, thick hedges surrounding her made it impossible to tell where it was coming from. One minute she'd spin expectantly, because she could swear the assassin had to be right behind her; the next brought her nothing but deep, dark silence.

She heard a sound and took a turn around a corner, but there was no one there. Still, she *knew* she'd heard something. "Elektra?" she asked tentatively. Her voice wasn't that loud because something wasn't right—she could *feel* it. "Is that you?" The leaves rustled again, and she looked up, then was horrified to watch the sides of two hedges go black, the leaves shriveling and falling away as the heavy foliage died right in front of her eyes. A moment later a shadowy figure stepped from between their twig-choked skeletons.

"Guess again."

And Abby looked into the white face of Typhoid Mary and saw death waiting in the woman's black, black eyes. . . .

Elektra had almost made it to Abby when Kirigi stepped out of the shadows in front of her.

They stared at each other, and Elektra knew the time to run was over. He had destroyed her weapons back at the mansion and now she was defenseless; finally she and Kirigi would meet their destiny, and finish the ongoing war between them—and a lot sooner than expected.

Or so he thought.

He came toward her, his katanas singing on the night breeze. She arched backward and waited just long enough for him to drive forward, then dove under his outstretched arm and through the now-rickety structure that held up the roof over the well. Her body grazed the decrepit posts and the whole thing shuddered at the impact; half-rotted shingles pattered against her back and dropped into the hole of blackness she had once thought held the secrets to her future. But that secret wasn't inside the well, it was *outside*, and Elektra knew just where to aim.

She hit the ground hands first, like a diver splitting the ocean's water and searching for that all-important underwater treasure. Her fingers went deep into the soft earth, pushing aside the grass and soil and closing firmly around the sais she had buried there so many years before. The metal felt warm and right across her palm, comfortable—she hadn't touched them since she was a child, yet it seemed as those these weapons were made so well they were already like a part of her. She pulled them out and rolled, then held them up triumphantly and turned to face Kirigi yet again.

He wasn't there.

"Those old things?" His voice was behind her, but not—overhead, to her left, everywhere.

"They won't save you."

This time Elektra saw him as he came toward her, his tar-pit eyes smiling and hungry, like a hyena coming in for the kill. He might have even laughed. A few yards away, Kirigi whirled his katanas, a pair of long, incredible weapons that had probably been lovingly fashioned by a swordsman long before Kirigi's birth. Their silver blades sparkled in moonlight broken by the intermittent clouds blowing across the sky, making them go from silver to black and back again. She was recovered enough now that Kirigi was being a little more cautious as he approached her, and the two of them extended their blades reflexively, judging their distance—Kirigi's were longer and she would need to remember her shorter range. When the edges met, the impact sent bright showers of red, yellow, and blue flying about their heads, like children wielding oddly shaped, deadly sparklers.

Elektra and Kirigi circled each other around the stone structure that had been built for her much younger self, swinging and parrying, dancing beneath and between the blades whistling across the air. Kirigi slashed and Elektra slipped beneath the edge, flipping her sais in midair and slamming them backward. But Kirigi was never there, and she pushed harder, growing more and more desperate in spite of her training and her instinct, wanting to stop this man and ensure, once and for all, that he would never get to young Abby.

While she sweated and strained, Kirigi, on the other hand, remained unaffected; the dark-haired man struck and blocked, staying calm and watching her face as they fought, as though he were searching for something.

"You're slipping, Elektra," Kirigi said, and his voice had an echoing, hollow quality that made it sound as if it was coming from somewhere else . . . perhaps from the very dreams he had just asked about. "Come on, now. Push, push. *Push!*"

Her father's words!

Panting now, Elektra kept striking at Kirigi, but her moves were slowing and her accuracy was suffering badly. Memories from her childhood flashed through her mind, interrupting her vision and making it impossible for her to properly judge where her enemy was. She tried to make her body flow naturally, but the blows were off—she was missing and Kirigi was playing with her, the way a cruel cat toys with a mouse before the final kill. She saw her father again at the pool, hammering his knowledge into her brain, insisting she train harder, work harder; his expression was hard and determined, she *would* do it right, or he would not let her rest. Then she saw herself in happier times, running along the estate and working her way through the maze, over and over again until she had conquered it. This was the only thing she'd ever truly had patience for in her youth. She saw—

She saw—

Herself as a child, struggling desperately in the swimming pool, tasting the heavy chlorine in her mouth and sputtering as she nearly drowned when pitted against the unrelenting discipline of her father's swimming lesson.

She saw—

Her mother's murder.

This vision, that one of all things, made Elektra lose herself, just for a moment. She swung too wide and Kirigi grinned and easily stepped out of range. Then, before she could recover and bring her sais back into position, he spun in a vicious double circle and came out of it with a side kick that caught her dead center on her sternum. One moment Elektra was ready to cut Kirigi into a thousand pieces; the next moment, Kirigi's kick had hurled her twenty feet backward down the heavily leafed path.

Elektra slammed viciously against the side of the old wishing well, then slid painfully down to the ground. The impact took the wind out of her, leaving her chest feeling like a balloon with a hole punched in it—small and depleted, void of any capacity to again hold oxygen. The flesh on her back screamed where the leather had ridden up and exposed her skin to the scouring effects of the stonework.

Elektra's chest hitched uselessly, then she toppled over and lay twitching on the ground. Kirigi's effortless leap took him directly over her, and there was nothing she could do but lie there and wait, blinking up at him through helpless, hopeless eyes as he raised his katanas and prepared to make the killing blow.

Somewhere on the other side of eternity, her father and mother waited. Elektra used her last bit of strength to spread her arms, then she waited, inviting death and just wanting it to, finally, be over.

Abby backed away from the Japanese death woman, but her lack of knowledge about Elektra's maze had sabotaged her and she was trapped in a dead end. Behind her back and on both sides were the twisted and dead remains of hedges several feet taller than her head; they were like walls of wooden barbed wires, sharp and deadly, impenetrable without a bladed weapon. There was nowhere to go and nothing to do but fight, and Abby knew instinctively that she *had* to keep Typhoid away from her. With no other way to defend herself, Abby brought up her chains and spun them expertly, cutting across the air with painful speed as she struggled to maintain a safety zone between her and Typhoid Mary.

But Typhoid wasn't concerned about the chains. With a speed that made Abby gasp, the woman reached forward, directly into the path of both chains, and let them wrap around her slender wrists and fingers. The force of their spinning stopped, and while anyone else would have screamed and gone to their knees, Typhoid only gave the chains a bland smile. Before Abby could yank backward, her weapons began to dissolve—blood-colored rust sped across the links right in front of Abby's dismayed gaze, freezing her in place. The metal corroded and cracked, the damage climbing up the chains and making them fall away to nothing but old, red powder in mere seconds.

Abby was defenseless.

The raven-haired woman look down at her hands, then lightly slapped them together to rid herself of the reddish dust coating her skin. It drifted to the ground and topped off a tiny pile—the remains of Abby's kusari-fundos—that was the color of powdered blood. Typhoid gave Abby a wistful look. "You know," she said, "*I* used to be the treasure." She cocked her head and listened for a moment, and Abby realized with a start that while she had previously been able to hear the sounds of the battle raging between Elektra and Kirigi on the other side of the hedge to Typhoid's right, the noise was gone. Now there was only a deep, unnerving silence.

Typhoid focused again on Abby and gave her a placid, black-lipped smile. Her voice was silky and slow. "Let's keep this between you and me."

Abby crouched, her face grim. She was just as good with her hands as she was with her chains, and she was determined to fight to the ground if she had to. In fact, she still felt confident enough about her skills to motion at the woman, daring her to come close enough to where Abby could land a few blows.

But no, Typhoid Mary had other plans for her, and Abby could only watch helplessly as the evil woman raised one palm and used the night's breeze to blow her the first of her poison-soaked kisses.

Oh no—Abby blinked hard and tried to hold her breath, but it was already too late. By the time Typhoid wandered over to gather Abby into her arms, Abby was sagging, already filled with fever and losing her fight for life.

Elektra let her head loll to the side, welcoming the feel of the rotting leaves against her cheek, the moistness of the soil. Soon she would be one with Mother Earth, her body reintegrated into the circle of life and eternity. As for the here and now . . . she didn't want to see Kirigi kill her—just let it be over with, let the blades do their work. She already knew how it would be—had she not already experienced exactly this at the hands of Bullseye? A magnificent flash of pain, a minute that would seem to last forever, then . . . blackness.

Yes, she could do that.

But through the decades, the lack of attention had taken its toll on the maze in more areas than those apparent at first glance. Now there were gaps beneath the hedges where the mounds of rotting leaves had eaten away chunks of the hedge structure with them, where the heavy spring and fall storm winds had blown aside the dry and more fragile piles of leaf debris. Typhoid Mary's touch had finished off the one directly in her line of sight, reducing most of its bottom to little more than dried and blackened twigs and leaving skull-sized gaps between it and the ground.

"Elektra . . ."

It was Abby's whispering voice, but . . . not. Elektra's blurring vision tried to focus almost against her own will, and—*there*.

Was she really seeing this, or was it kimagure? She couldn't be sure—she was unfocused, weak, at the worst she had ever been in a battle. Even so, she could not ignore what was playing out in front of her eyes, whether it was reality or what might be in only a few very short minutes.

Held tightly in Typhoid's embrace, the girl had

sagged to the ground just on the other side of the hedge. Her head was thrown back but her eyes were open and staring right at Elektra. Typhoid Mary was rocking her like a dying infant; with her black lips nearly touching the side of Abby's head, she was crooning some misbegotten death song into the teenager's ear. Abby's hands were lying palm-up on the ground, the fingers twitching feebly.

NO!

There had been little in Elektra's life that had touched her heart since the double strike of losing her father and enduring a death that had parted her from Matt Murdock. This girl, and to a lesser degree her father, had done just that—reawakened something blocked away and forced to stay dormant for too long. That segregation had served Elektra well, given her time to heal and a solid measure of self-protection, but the time for such things was over now.

She would *not* let Abby Miller die because of the Hand.

Above her, Kirigi's smile had stretched to a self-satisfied rictus. "Here ends the lesson!" he said triumphantly. He raised his katanas as high as he could, gripping their handles tightly. Elektra inhaled deeply and stretched her arms over her head as if she were preparing for death, even welcoming it. But the second before Kirigi brought down his blades, Elektra's fingers closed around the hilt of the sais she had dropped when she'd hit the side of the well. She swung up at the same time Kirigi swung down. Their weapons met with a head-ringing CLANG!—

—and Kirigi's katanas shattered.

He had a millisecond to look stupidly at the remains of his broken swords, then Elektra's right sai pierced the center of his chest.

He tripped backward as Elektra's momentum pulled her up and propelled her toward him, his wide, black gaze going from Elektra to the blade buried in his heart as if he couldn't believe such a thing could actually happen, not to him, not to *Kirigi*.

But Elektra only stared at him grimly as she pulled from deep inside herself, gathering every bit of strength she had and lifting the killer overhead using her two deadly blades. "The lesson is over," she said coldly, "when the student becomes the master."

Kirigi's body wobbled over her head, then she flung him as hard as she could, right into the wishing well. For a second, there was nothing, then suddenly the familiar noxious smoke spewed from the well's shadowed opening like a shower of toxic fireworks. Elektra yanked her face away and threw up one arm to protective her eyes as a swirl of nearly blinding green fire exploded from the well.

The sais that had killed Kirigi lay on the ground at Elektra's feet. What she had seen had been reality, not kimagure, and now Elektra saw that Typhoid Mary had gone; satisfied that her evil work was done, the woman had left Abby lying motionless on the other side of the desiccated hedge. Waving away the last of the smelly smoke, Elektra bent and picked up her weapons, sensing the air and everything around her with a flow of inner peace that was steadier than anything she'd experienced in years. She brought up one sai on her palm and closed her eyes, then twirled it twice and threw it as hard as she could. When she opened her eyes, Elektra saw the sai whirling away end over end, burning its way through the dead hedges as it went in the opposite direction from Abby. Elektra smiled darkly just as she saw Typhoid Mary turn the corner ahead.

The sai slid neatly into the small space between the poisonous woman's eyebrows.

Other than that it rivaled Kirigi's spectacular end, Elektra barely remembered the explosion and the burning that followed the death of Typhoid Mary. Abby was the only thing in the world now that was important, and she was at the teenager's side in seconds after slicing through the dead brush that stood between them. But Abby was almost gone, her breathing so shallow Elektra could barely feel it against her cheek when she bent close to the girl's face. The teenager's skin was china-white, a bizarre mirror image of Typhoid's own Noh mask.

"Abby," Elektra said urgently, "concentrate. Focus

on your breathing." Sweat and steam poured off the prone body, but there was no sign that she could hear Elektra's instructions. Elektra's hands gripped Abby's wrists. "Listen to me!" Elektra's voice rose as she fought to control her own panic. "Use my voice as a guide—" Before she could continue, Abby jerked, then convulsed in Elektra's arms. Her cheeks, so pale just a moment ago, flushed bright red as the fever climbed to its highest point yet, then her eyes, still slightly open, rolled back in her head until only the whites showed—

—and her breathing stopped entirely.

Elektra clutched at Abby's shoulders, then shook her. "Don't die!" she cried. "Abby, please don't—slow your heart! Slow the poison!"

But Abby only lay there, still and silent. Elektra searched for a pulse, but there was nothing. She searched again, refusing to give up. "No! No! Abby—come back. *Abby, come back!*"

For the first time since she had mistakenly plunged her sai into Daredevil's shoulder and nearly killed him, Elektra cried. And as the tears ran down her face, she gathered Abby in her arms and sprinted for the house.

Elektra remembered.

She remembered being a young girl and coming down the upstairs hallway, how her footsteps had made muffled thumping noises along the long, expensive Persian carpet runner. She remembered standing before the closed bedroom door and how tall it seemed, how she had to crane her neck to see above it where the wall and the sixteen-foot ceiling met. Worse than that, she remembered opening the door itself and seeing her mother's body lying on the bed. In this memory, the *real* one, her mother was still dead, but the blood from the nearly hidden wound was minimal and there was no demon shrieking at her as it escaped out the window. There was only her mother's corpse and the blackclad ninja, a figure with which she would become intimately familiar over the course of her life. Yes, her mother had died in this bedroom—

The same room, and the same bed, in which Abby now lay.

As she had done over her mother so many years ago, Elektra hovered over Abby tonight. Elektra could only guess, of course, but even though the tools were different, perhaps this was the same way the two ambulance attendants, those luckless, surprised New York City employees, had watched over her as she'd died under their care.

As she was doing to Abby, Stick had done to her.

It was the way of the warrior.

Doing this for Abby now, Elektra realized she had missed something all these years, and she had started by missing it all the way back when she had trained under Stick in the hidden compound. There was no doubt in her mind that the love, knowledge, and energy flowing from her into this child had come to her in the same way from her mentor, Stick. Had she not been so self-centered and blind to the world around her, so full of rage over the hand that destiny had dealt her, she might have seen that—she might have seen a *lot* of things. Her fingertips touched Abby's head, arms, legs, and all the while she whispered in the teenager's ear, putting herself into the healing, inserting her undeniable will into Abby's already strong spirit. Her voice was soft and songlike, crooning, and she would not stop, not now, not ever, until she had found her way right down into Abby's soul.

"Hey you, warrior girl." Elektra could see her breath tickling the soft hairs against Abby's temple and she willed Abby to feel what she saw, to experience the sensation of the strands of hair sliding across her sensitive skin. "Do you see me? Look at me, I'm over here. No, no—right here." She squeezed Abby's wrists, pushing her silent commands into the flesh rather than trying to feel for life. "That's it," she continued in a murmur. "Now come to me, come to me, come here. Obey your superiors, that's right. Always obey your superiors."

Elektra paused, knowing she would start again if she had to, she would *not* give up. Abby's face was still blank, but . . . *yes!* There *was* something . . . something . . .

She looked down. One of Abby's fingers had moved

until it was just barely touching Elektra's own. Coincidence? No—suddenly Abby gagged, then her body twisted on the bed. She writhed and turned, but Elektra made no attempt to hold or quiet her other than to keep her grip on the teenager's wrists. It was a terrible thing to watch, but some things in this universe were meant to be done alone.

Coming back to life would not be any easier for Abby than it had been for Elektra years before.

It had taken more than half an hour for the convulsions to subside, and now the exhausted Abby was sleeping quietly. Elektra was content to just sit at Abby's bedside and listen to her breathing, watch her chest rise up and down and monitor the tiny jump of her not-so-strong pulse beneath the fragile skin of her neck.

It was almost ten when Elektra heard Mark's crutch-aided footsteps thunking down the hallway, followed by the much more subtle stride she recognized as Stick. In his haste, Mark came around the doorway and jerked to a stop, nearly falling when he saw his daughter's prone figure on the bed. Elektra waved her hand to call him in when she saw the fear on his face.

"She's fine," Elektra said. "She's *fine*." She rose and gestured again for Mark to take her place by the bedside. She met Stick's blind gaze, then walked to the window and looked outside. She had not stood at this window since well before her mother's death, but finally, after all this time, she had found the sense of detachment—if not peace—she needed from her mother's passing.

The demon in her dreams was just that . . .

A dream.

Elektra couldn't exactly recall the last time she'd been in the master bedroom and seen the sunshine spilling through the tall windows, but it was sure doing that now. It was fitting, though, a lovely morning to welcome Abby back into the land of the living and into a life free of those who had tried so hard to kill her and her father. Mark was in parental hover mode, of course, and Stick stood regally in the doorway as Elektra went over to the bed.

She smiled down at Abby. "How are you?"

Abby nodded—better—but she wasn't quite ready to try her voice. After a moment, Elektra sat on the side of the bed, then she jumped a little when Abby reached over and took her hand. She didn't pull away.

"So," Elektra said after a bit, "what's next?" Abby looked at her with a frown, not understanding. "Kirigi's gone," Elektra reminded her. "No one's after you. You can do what you want now." Abby's frown deepened and Elektra almost shook her head as she realized how strange it must be for Abby to actually have a *choice* in what she could now do with her life. No one had ever revealed the specifics, but she and her father must have been running for a long, long time. Elektra grinned. "Back to school?" This question made the girl scrunch up her face so much that Elektra chuckled. She gestured toward the blind man. "Train with Stick?" This time Abby looked undecided, so Elektra decided to lighten things up all the way. "Go lie on a beach and get a tan," she said with cheerful finality.

Abby considered this, then looked hopefully toward her dad. "I want ice cream," she ventured in a scratchy voice. Both Mark and Elektra laughed, then without warning Abby threw her arms around Elektra and held on tight.

Elektra swallowed, fighting against tears. She was supposed to be the strong mentor here, not a sappy friend. It would be nice if she could be both, but her life just wasn't set up like that. The girl's next words were a bittersweet reminder of exactly that. "You gave me my life back," Abby whispered.

"You gave me mine," Elektra said in return, and she meant it.

Only Abby heard her, but it was enough to make the girl sit back and stare at her with a sudden understanding that was a little too old for her years. Tears glistened in the teenager's eyes. "Will I see you again?"

On the other side of the bed, Mark sat up straighter on his chair. "Are you leaving?"

Elektra smiled at them both. "We'll find each other."

She hugged Abby, then gave her a gentle kiss on the forehead. Over Abby's head, her gaze met Mark's. His was hopeful, hers was forgiving. The reconciliation was complete . . . but they both knew it would never go any further.

Elektra left the estate feeling better about life and herself than she had since the death of her father and her parting from Matt. She stopped outside for a while, looking at the ruins of the maze and the remains of the overgrown grounds. What would become of this place now? What *should* become of it? She had so much history here, but Elektra wasn't sure she ever wanted to return, or what she would do if she did. Yes, she had some decisions to make, but she would take her time about it. They would not be made lightly.

"Please," she finally said to Stick. "Don't let her be like me." She'd known he was behind her for at least three minutes.

Stick made his way carefully forward until he was standing by her side. "Why not? You haven't turned out so bad."

She glanced sideways at him, surprised at the tone of approval in his voice. They'd crossed attitudes so often that it was something she'd never thought she'd hear. "I . . . just don't want it to be so hard for her," she finally said.

But her mentor simply shrugged. "That's up to her."

Elektra could only lift a corner of her mouth rue-fully—that was all too true. "Anyway," she added, "your second life's never like your first, is it?"

Stick smiled vaguely. "Sometimes it's better."

Elektra looked at him and knew that even though the man didn't have his vision, he could see her.

She turned and walked away, knowing that he always would.

DEADLOCK.

Roshi sat back and studied the Go board. "You played well, as usual," he said.

Stick leaned forward and let his fingers touch lightly across the board, feeling the pieces along the playing field, finding and mentally recording his white ones. "Not too shabby yourself. Unfortunately, I lost that treasure you so coveted."

"The little one—she died after all? So sorry." Roshi paused, then nodded sadly. His eyes glittered in the mellow light of the room. "And I have lost my greatest warrior, the magnificent Kirigi."

"Who tried to displace you as leader," Stick pointed out.

Roshi grinned and raised one eyebrow. "And somehow failed to kill the girl you try to convince me is dead." He turned to a small table off to the side and ceremoniously poured two cups of sake. Stick accepted one and they lifted their cups toward each other.

"Yet once again," Roshi added, "for all our skill, we

end in a stalemate. What is the point of playing if no one wins?"

Now it was Stick's turn to smile. "Just to keep playing, I suppose."

They finished their sake without saying anything else, then both men reached out calloused fingers and began meticulously gathering their stones. Oddly enough, it almost seemed as if they were "unplaying" their game, reversing all the maneuverings and situations that had already taken place.

Roshi looked down at the board when it was finally cleared. He seemed vaguely puzzled, as if he were still asking himself why bother. "Another game, then?"

After a moment, Stick reached out and carefully placed the first white stone on the board.

THE END . . . ?